SHUTTER BUG

Richard Baran

Mouse Gate™
1103 Middlecreek
Friendswood, Texas 77546
281-992-3131   281-482-5390 Fax
www.totalrecallpress.com

Copyright © 2016 by: Richard Baran
Edited by William R. "Will" Barshop
Copy Editors: Carol Fredrickson and Joseph "Bucky" Baran
www.buckbaran.com
All rights reserved

ISBN: 978-1-59095-316-7
UPC: 6-43977-43169-1
Library of Congress Control Number: 2015954557

Printed in the United States of America with simultaneous printings in Australia, Canada, and United Kingdom.

FIRST EDITION
1   2   3   4   5   6   7   8   9   10

To: A. M. D. G.

Author Richard Baran

holds a doctorate and two masters' degrees besides his bachelor's in business. A Navy veteran, he taught and coached for forty years at the secondary school and collegiate levels. His publishing credits include, a coaching text, *Coaching Football's Polypotent Offense* a short story, *That Ain't No Walleye*, and several dozen articles in professional journals.

Baran's first novel, *The Jacket*, was published by Total Recall Press as were his subsequent novels, *Where Have All The Go-Go's Gone? Part One; When Will They Ever Learn—Where Have All The Go-Go's Gone? Part Two, Shutter Bug, Heroes and Idles, Did You Boo Hopalong Cassidy*.and *The Dutchman's Gift*.

Dick and his eighth grade sweetheart, Carol, have eighteen grandchildren and they divide their year between Franklin Park, Illinois; Phoenix, Arizona and Minocqua, Wisconsin.

Visit www.richardbaran.com for more information.

About The Book

Emma Grace Waveland, a self-proclaimed Shutter Bug at twelve, finds herself transported from a safari in Disney World to Africa's Serengeti where she joins a group of professional hunters who capture wild animals for zoos. Her new adventure brings her face-to-face with deadly crocodiles, a giant rhino, a pet rock python, a lady photographer who looks like a young version of her great grandmother, hunters who resemble old movie stars and a camp cook with mysterious powers. Her family doesn't believe her when she returns from her trip, but she has evidence on her cameras' memory cards and her iPhone.

Serengeti

From Wikipedia, the free encyclopedia

For other uses, see <u>Serengeti (disambiguation)</u>.

Map of Tanzania showing national parks

The **Serengeti** (/ˌsɛrən'gɛti/) ecosystem is a geographical region in Africa. It is located in north <u>Tanzania</u> and extends to south-western <u>Kenya</u> between latitudes 1 and 3 degrees south latitude and 34 and 36 degrees east longitude. It spans approximately 30,000 km² (12,000 sq mi). The Kenyan part of the Serengeti is known as <u>Maasai Mara</u>.

The Serengeti hosts the largest terrestrial mammal <u>migration</u>

in the world, which helps secure it as one of the <u>Seven Natural Wonders of Africa</u>[1] and one of the <u>ten natural travel wonders of the world</u>.[2] The Serengeti is also renowned for its large lion population and is one of the best places to observe prides in their natural environment.[3] The region contains the <u>Serengeti National Park</u> in Tanzania and several <u>game reserves</u>.

Approximately 70 larger <u>mammal</u> and 500 <u>bird</u> species are found there. This high diversity is a function of diverse habitats, including riverine forests, <u>swamps</u>, <u>kopjes</u>, grasslands, and woodlands.[4] <u>Blue wildebeests</u>, <u>gazelles</u>, <u>zebras</u>, and <u>buffalos</u> are some of the commonly found large mammals in the region.

There has been controversy about a <u>proposed road to be built through the Serengeti</u>.[5]

Serengeti is derived from the <u>Maasai language</u>, Maa; specifically, "Serengit" meaning "Endless Plains".[6][7]

Contents

History

Much of the Serengeti was known to outsiders as Maasailand. The <u>Maasai</u> are known as fierce warriors and live alongside most wild animals with an aversion to eating game and birds, subsisting exclusively on their cattle. Historically, their strength and reputation kept the newly arrived Europeans from exploiting the animals and resources of most of their land. A <u>rinderpest epidemic</u> and drought during the 1890s greatly reduced the numbers of both Maasai and animal populations.

The Tanzanian government later in the 20th century re-settled the Maasai around the Ngorongoro Crater. Poaching and the absence of fires, which had been the result of human activity, set the stage for the development of dense woodlands and thickets over the next 30–50 years. Tsetse fly populations now prevented any significant human settlement in the area.

By the mid-1970s, wildebeest and the Cape buffalo populations had recovered and were increasingly cropping the grass, reducing the amount of fuel available for fires.[8] The reduced intensity of fires has allowed Acacia to once again become established.[9]

Great migration

Migrating wildebeests

Each year around the same time, the circular great wildebeest migration begins in the Ngorongoro Conservation Area of the southern Serengeti in Tanzania. This migration is a natural phenomenon determined by the availability of grazing. This phase lasts from approximately January to March, when the calving season begins – a time when there is plenty of rain-ripened grass available for the 260,000 zebra that precede 1.7 million wildebeest and the following hundreds of thousands of other plains game, including around 470,000 gazelles.[10][11][12]

Wildebeests crossing the river during the Serengeti migration

During February, the wildebeest spend their time on the short grass plains of the southeastern part of the ecosystem, grazing and giving birth to approximately 500,000 calves within a 2 to 3-week period. Few calves are born ahead of time and of these, hardly any survive. The main reason is that very young calves are more noticeable to predators when mixed with older calves from the previous year. As the rains end in May, the animals start moving northwest into the areas around the Grumeti River, where they typically remain until late June. The crossings of the Grumeti and Mara rivers beginning in July are a popular safari attraction because crocodiles are lying in wait.[10] The herds arrive in Kenya in late July / August, where they stay for the remainder of the dry season, except that the Thomson's and <u>Grant's Gazelles</u> move only east/west. In early November, with the start of the short rains the migration starts moving south again, to the short grass plains of the southeast, usually arriving in December in plenty of time for calving in February.[13]

About 250,000 wildebeest die during the journey from Tanzania to the <u>Maasai Mara National Reserve</u> in southwestern Kenya, a total of 800 kilometers (500 mi). Death is usually from thirst, hunger, exhaustion, or <u>predation</u>.[2]

Ecology

Lioness on a kopje, or rock outcropping

Masai Giraffe in <u>Serengeti National Park</u>, Tanzania

River and the Serengeti plains

The Serengeti has some of East Africa's finest game areas.[14] The governments of Tanzania and Kenya maintain a number of protected areas, including national parks, conservation areas, and game reserves, that give legal protection to over 80 percent of the Serengeti.[4]

The southeastern area lies in the rain shadow of the Ngorongoro Conservation Area's highlands and is composed of shortgrass treeless plains with abundant small dicots. Soils are high in nutrients, overlying a shallow calcareous hardpan. A gradient of soil depth northwestward across the plains results in changes in the herbaceous community and taller grass. About 70 kilometers (43 mi) west, Acacia woodlands appear suddenly and stretch west to Lake Victoria and north to the Loita Plains, north of the Maasai Mara National Reserve. The sixteen Acacia species vary over this range, their distribution determined by edaphic conditions and soil depth. Near Lake Victoria, flood plains have developed from ancient lakebeds.

In the far northwest, Acacia woodlands are replaced by broadleaved Terminalia-Combretum woodlands, caused by a change in geology. This area has the highest rainfall in the system and forms a refuge for the migrating ungulates at the end of the dry season.[15][16]

Altitudes in the Serengeti range from 920 to 1,850 meters (3,020 to 6,070 ft) with mean temperatures varying from 15 to 25 °C (59 to 77 °F). Although the climate is usually warm and dry, rainfall occurs in two rainy seasons: March to May, and a shorter season in October and November. Rainfall amounts vary from a low of 508 millimeters (20 in) in the lee of the Ngorongoro highlands to a high of 1,200 millimeters (47 in) on the shores of Lake Victoria.[17] The highlands, which are considerably cooler than the plains and are covered by montane forest, mark the eastern border of the basin in which the Serengeti lies.

The Serengeti Plain is punctuated by granite and gneiss

outcroppings known as kopjes. These outcroppings are the result of volcanic activity. Kopjes provide a microhabitat for non-plains wildlife. One kopje likely to be seen by visitors to the Serengeti is the Simba Kopje (Lion Kopje). The Serengeti was used as inspiration for the animated Disney feature film *The Lion King* and subsequent theatrical production.

The area is also home to the Ngorongoro Conservation Area, which contains Ngorongoro Crater and the Olduvai Gorge, where some of the oldest hominid fossils have been found.

See also

Wikimedia Commons has media related to *Serengeti*.

- Tanzania
- List of topics related to Africa
- Maasai mythology

References

1. Seven Natural Wonders of Africa
2. Partridge, Frank (20 May 2006). "The fast show". *The Independent (London)*. Retrieved 2007-03-14.
3. Nolting, Mark (2012). *Africa's Top Wildlife Countries*. Global Travel Publishers Inc. p. 356. ISBN 978-0939895151.
4. http://www.ath.aegean.gr/srcosmos/showpub.aspx?aa=8868[dead link]
5. [1]
6. Briggs, Phillip (2006), *Northern Tanzania: The Bradt Safari Guide with Kilimanjaro and Zanzibar*, Bradt Travel Guides, p. 198, ISBN 978-1-84162-146-3
7. "Maa (Maasai) Dictionary". Darkwing.uoregon.edu. Retrieved 2010-10-23.
8. Morell, Virginia (1997), "Return of the Forest", *Science* **278** (5346): 2059, doi:10.1126/science.278.5346.2059

9. Sinclair, Anthony Ronald Entrican; Arcese, Peter, eds. (1995). *Serengeti II: Dynamics, Management, and Conservation of an Ecosystem*. University of Chicago Press. pp. 73–76. ISBN 978-0-226-76032-2. Retrieved 2010-10-23.

10. Anouk Zijlma. "The Great Annual Wildlife Migration – The Great Migration of Wildebeest and Zebra". About.com. Retrieved 3 June 2014.

11. "How to Get There, Ngorongoro Crater". Ngorongoro Crater Tanzania. 2013. Retrieved 3 June 2014.

12. "Ngorongoro Conservation Area". United Nations Educational, Scientific and Cultural Organization – World Heritage Centre. Retrieved 3 June 2014.

13. Croze, Harvey; Mari, Carlo; Estes, Richard D. (2000). *Serengeti's Great Migration*. Abbeville Press. ISBN 978-0-789-20669-5.

14. Pavitt, Nigel (2001), *Africa's Great Rift Valley*, Harry N. Abrams, p. 122, ISBN 978-0-8109-0602-0

15. Sinclair, A. R. E.; Mduma, Simon A. R.; Fryxell, John M. (2008), *Serengeti III: Human Impacts on Ecosystem Dynamics*, Chicago: University of Chicago Press, p. 11, ISBN 978-0-226-76033-9

16. Sinclair, A. R. E.; Mduma, S. A.; Hopcraft, J. G.; Fryxell, J. M.; Hilborn, R.; Thirgood, S. (2007), "Long-Term Ecosystem Dynamics in the Serengeti: Lessons for Conservation" (PDF), *Conservation Biology* **21** (3): 580–590, doi:10.1111/j.1523-1739.2007.00699.x

17. "The Serengeti National Park". Glcom.com. Retrieved 2010-10-23.

Chapter 1

Emmy idolized her great grandmother even though she had never seen the relative who died decades before Emmy was born. Granna Ellie, as she was known, had been famous. At least that's what the stories had said and Emmy knew them all, treating each one with reverence.

Most kids only know stories about their great grandparents. Emmy heard lots of stories, her Granna Ellie's name bantered about; sometime humor was attached, other mentions were serious, words like tough and tenacious used to describe her. The expression Emmy liked the most was, "A real sweetheart." That came from Emmy's father. She also heard about several episodes describing her Granna Ellie's work as a professional press photographer. There were things like flashbulbs popping and ugly reactions from some people who didn't want their picture taken. Emmy had also heard stories that bordered on the macabre. Those episodes dealt with the insane cruelty and bloody carnage of war. Emmy remembered every word of those stories. A pile of photographs, some cracked and faded, had been sandwiched in with the family yarns and Emmy absorbed and cherished each one. What she cherished, even worshipped, was a special keepsake of her Granna Ellie. Emmy's father had told her that it was a prize from a box of Cracker Jack.

"I don't know why she kept that old plastic piece of junk," Emmy's father had said to her, sliding the small red blue figure of what looked like a sailor boy across the dinner table. "The back is all scratched up," he continued, sounding bored. He turned it over. "See," he said, trying to sound like an authority on Cracker Jack prizes. "The back of that prize has several circles looking like gouges dug into it."

Emmy saw where her father's index finger mockingly pointed at the flawed reverse side of the sailor boy. She saw it right away and what she saw weren't scratches or defects. The three circles, one large and two much smaller sitting on top of the larger one weren't a mistake. Emmy couldn't wait to get to her bedroom and examine the special gift that had once belonged to her Granna Ellie. She would keep the gift forever and remember her great grandmother's memory for all eternity.

Granna Ellie died when Emmy's father was twelve, the same age as Emmy. There was nothing forgetful either about Emma Grace Waveland. She went by the name Emmy and was smart beyond her years, looking and acting, according to her father, exactly like her Granna Ellie. "Our daughter's going to grow up to be a liberated female rebel just like that grandmother of mine," her father said.

Emma's father, Walt, had attached several pet nicknames to his daughter. She was Emmy or Gracie, her mother also adopting Gracie because Grace had been her mother's name. Emmy Lou was used by Emma's father because of his love for Emmy Lou Harris, the country singer. His latest name for his daughter, one her mother detested, was Bugs, short for Shutter Bug.

"She's a darned clone of my grandmother," her father had

remarked after seeing his toddler pick up a battered Kodak Baby Brownie camera unceremoniously tossed at her feet by her older brother, Joshua. He had been amazed that she didn't hurl the scarred, old black plastic relic her brother had found while searching for treasures in the attic crawl space in their house. She managed to toss everything else that made the mistake of getting within her reach.

"Here, you little brat," Josh had said, dumping the camera at her feet. "Don't choke on it."

The entire family was surprised that Emmy didn't fling the camera back at her brother after trying to stuff the Baby Brownie into her mouth. She crammed anything she could get her tiny hands on into her drooling mouth. What mesmerized her father was watching his daughter place the viewfinder to her right eye as if photography had been her profession, her tiny index finger clicking the silver colored shutter release located under the lens. Walt Waveland, his soothing Caribbean blue eyes sparkling, grinned and said to his wife, Betty, "She's just like her great grandmother, a darned shutter bug. The next thing we know she'll be in some exotic, far off land taking pictures for National Geographic."

Several years later, Walt Waveland couldn't believe what he had witnessed. Film had gone into the Kodak Brownie; lots of film. Her father had located a rare photography shop that still developed film. What came back in the envelope after the film was developed were not pictures. Each was the portrait of a gifted artist. "The kid's incredible," he said to Emmy's mother. "These look like they should be on the cover of Life magazine," he said. "Didn't her great grandmother have one of her pictures on the cover of Life?" More and more rolls of film were developed. Then a triple package of prints came back from the printer. Walt Waveland flipped the pictures onto the front seat of the family SUV into a pile after a quick look. His head went from side-to-side as he picked up the pictures, stuffing them all into one envelope and then letting out a boisterous, out-of-character laugh. He entered the house through the garage and strolled into the kitchen where he saw his wife. "Look at all of the pictures our Emmy took of that worn out shaggy pony at Kiddie Land." He grinned. "Dang, she's just got out of kindergarten," he said, amazed. "She was the only kid in the entire place with a camera. She took all kinds of pictures of that horse; even crawled underneath for different angles. Didn't care about dirt or manure or let anything get in her way. The only time she stopped was to put more film in her camera. She didn't care if she got up in that saddle and went for a ride."

"Didn't you once tell me about her going off to take pictures for National Geographic?" Betty Waveland asked, her lips curled up but sealed to hide a line of slightly crooked lower teeth that made her self-conscious. "Count your blessings, Walt. Our daughter could be sending those so-called Selfie pictures of herself all over the world on the Internet like that poor friend of hers, Sally Ann. Gosh, oh golly, that child sure got herself in a load of trouble."

Walt nodded. "Twelve years old and painted up like a twenty year old woman of questionable moral turpitude," he said, pausing and thinking for a moment. "And, what was the word you used?" he asked. "Oh, yeah, poor child," he continued then pausing again. "I think the kid was an idiot."

"Oh, Walt, no child is an idiot."

"Okay," replied Walt. "Sally Ann is not an idiot. She just acts like one." He took a deep breath then said, "The kid's mother, however, is the prototype for village idiots the world over what with her rationalized lame excuses, finger pointing and blaming the world for her daughter's colossal screw ups."

Betty Waveland covered her mouth with an open hand as she laughed. "Like I said, Walt, count our blessings." She laughed again. "And while you're counting, I think you'd better start putting aside some of your paycheck so you can take your family on one of those exotic safaris so your daughter can take pictures."

"Go on a what?" he asked, the surprise in his voice seldom heard.

"Emma has already taken pictures of all of the animals at both the Lincoln Park and Brookfield Zoo's," Betty said. "Besides, I think she has all but attacked every single person walking a pet within eight square blocks of where we live asking to take pictures."

Walt's head went from side-to-side several times before he started to chuckle. "Yeah, can you see me on a safari? What was the name of that old John Wayne movie about capturing animals for zoos?" He thought for a moment. "Hatari, yeah, that was it." He smiled at his wife. "Can you see Emmy in Africa taking pictures of wild animals?" He broke into a grin. "Next thing you know she'll want to bring home a baby elephant for a pet." Laughter exploded from the grin. "And, after we get back from trekking through the jungle, you, my love, can address me as Bwana."

Betty barely shook her head. "Wonderful," she said, sounding exasperated. "Now I have a Bwana to join Emmy Lou, Gracie and Bugs."

Eleanor "Ellie" van Sestern had been held in the highest esteem by many of her fellow professional press photographers; most males admired, even envied her work, too many publicly shunned her. Those in her profession who mattered lauded her for her accomplishments.   There were scores of accolades heaped upon Granna Ellie and Emma Grace Waveland had memorized every well documented story. There was a quartet of bulging scrapbooks, each page filled with neatly mounted newspaper articles, certificates, citations, photographs and awards to prove that Eleanor van Sestern really did what she did. Each of the artifacts had been labeled with dates, locations and comments. Back before and during the World War II years, and for decades after, women were left in the shadows of the notoriety spotlight, those lights controlled by men. Eleanor van Sestern had saved the mementoes of her accomplishments from a relatively short but productive career. It was a career that was marked by fingers getting dirt under their nails and several of those nails snapping off as they clawed and dug in way too often in battle. A dozen shoe boxes held the proof until well after her death. Those memories eventually went from the shoe boxes to scrapbooks. Her incredible achievements with a camera had been assembled by Emmy's father, Walt after he and her mother had gone through the personal belongings of his late grandmother.

"Check all of those boxes in the closet," Emmy's mother had said excitedly while newlywed Walt Waveland groused. "This isn't exactly what I had in mind for our honeymoon," he said to his wife. "Cleaning out my grandmother's house doesn't exactly smell of romance," he grumbled in his native northern Wisconsin twang, the accent identifiable with growing up next door to Michigan's Upper Peninsula. "There ain't nothin' but a bunch of old papers and crap in dem dare boxes don't cha know." He held up a sheet of paper that looked like it had been rolled up into a ball and then ironed it out by dragging it over the chrome edge of the kitchen table where he sat, his wife seated opposite of him, her view blocked by stacks of boxes.

"Mmmm," he murmured. "Part of her divorce from dat first husband of hers," he said softly as if reflecting. "The marriage didn't last very long," he continued as he sifted through more papers. "Mmmm," he mouthed again, a sign of anger apparent. "Dat dare spineless coward used my grandmother for a punching bag before she dumped him and met my grandfather." Another, "Mmmm," came from him.

"Oh, Walt calm down," his wife said. "Let it go. Your grandmother married a nice man." His wife got up and went to the other side of the table and gently placed a hand on his shoulder.

Walt looked up and smiled at his bride. "Yeah, Grampa Chester was a nice man. Then they saw the letter. It had a picture of the White House embossed across the top. The letter was brief, written in long hand, perfect penmanship, the salutation stating: "My dear Ellie." Then they saw the first sentence and began having trouble breathing.

Bess and I would like to thank you for the beautiful photograph…

Their eyes stayed glued to the signature for what seemed forever before Walt Waveland muttered, "Holy crap. It's from dat Truman fella, the President of the United States." An anemic whistle escaped his lips.

That letter and many more like it, most from various Washington big wigs, appeared to be treated as if Eleanor van Sestern had discovered either the Dead Sea Scrolls or a local Wisconsin supper club that offered an all-you-can-eat Friday night fish fry specializing in Walleye. One by one each of the artifacts was glued on page after page of a scrapbook that newlyweds, Walt and Betty Waveland had bought that same day at a Ben Franklin store after discovering what they saw were treasures. Each gem was mounted on a page by the couple as if they were an operating room team performing a delicate surgery. Soon one scrapbook multiplied into a collection of four bulging volumes.

Emmy treated each scrapbook with reverence. All others including family members, her three brothers specifically, who wanted even a simple peek at the collection of treasures were threatened with a verbal warning, some form of physical violence or possible banishment to Siberia if a single page didn't receive treatment reserved for royalty or a Papal visit. Her three brothers were threatened with more if they didn't follow her instructions on how to turn each page. Soon, she was the only member of the Waveland family who was allowed to touch the books and her great grandmother became Emma Grace Waveland's idol, bigger than any rock star. There would never be another in her life.

It didn't take Emmy's father long to realize his daughter's penchant for photography exceeded that of being a whim or a passing fancy. Her special talent appeared to be genetic and a Kodak Baby Brownie camera a part of her DNA. "You took to that camera like it was life itself," her father had reminded her many times. "You started snapping imaginary pictures the moment your serious brown eyes found the view finder and your tiny fingers attacked that shutter." Now, as her father sat in his favorite chair, a forest green color Chesterfield style, Emmy sat on the arm nearest him. Her father laughed lovingly and put his arm around his daughter. "I don't know if you loved that camera as much as that Cracker Jack prize I gave you, the one that belonged to your great grandmother."

Emmy looked adoringly at her dad and felt his hand slide to her shoulder. "It was more than a Cracker Jack prize, Dad" she said. "It was magical and, I bet, Granna Ellie knew it was. That's why she kept it."

"Magical or not, it was the strangest Cracker Jack prize I ever saw," said her father, giving her shoulder a squeeze.

Emmy smiled, placed her hand on top of his and squeezed it in return. "Those scratched circles on the back of that prize were a picture of Mickey Mouse," she said, her eyes matching the seriousness of her statement.

"Okay, Emmy Lou, if you insist," her father said. "I still think those so called circles you call them were a mistake that was made when that sailor came out of that plastic mold."

Emmy's face radiated love for her father. "It's definitely Mickey Mouse, Daddy, and that prize is magical."

"Okay," her father said. "If you insist it's magical, it's magical." He broke into a grin. "Here's something else that's magical," he said, handing her a brown paper bag that looked like something her father used to take his lunch to work.

Her expression did the asking; the asking aided by the heavy weight of the bag.

"Your Brownie camera has seen better days," he said, watching his daughter's fingers gently tracing the shape inside the bag.

Emmy removed an old camera from the bag and didn't say a word. Her fingers Brailled the rectangular box shaped camera that had more handles, dials and lenses than she ever saw. Her eyes continued to ask.

"It's just like one of the cameras your great grandmother used to use," he said. "It's called a Rollieflex. It's not as fancy as these new digital things and there's no phone attached like the one your friend, Sally Ann uses, but, in its day, it was considered the Cadillac of cameras," he continued, beaming. "I found it at an estate sale."

"You said Granna Ellie used one just like this?" asked Emmy, her question barely audible.

Her father nodded. "I think you can still buy film," he said. "And you still have that darkroom I made for you down in the basement so you can develop it."

"Oh, Daddy," Emmy said, jumping up from the table and wrapping her arms around her father. "The first picture I take will be of you."

"Great," said her father. "One picture and you'll break the camera."

Emmy wasted no time in finding out about her camera. Google helped her. She devoured every word and picture that came up on her computer screen about the Rollieflex camera her father had given her. She appeared almost relentless in her pursuit and choice of subjects. Her Baby Brownie wasn't forgotten. It sat in a place of prominence on her night table shelf in her bedroom. Also not forgotten was the new digital camera her parents had given her for her birthday a year earlier. Somehow, the simplicity of pointing a camera, pushing down a button and seeing a picture in an instant couldn't compete with a light meter, f-stop setting and her belief in her special Cracker Jack prize depicting Mickey Mouse. She also believed that what Ellie van Sestern did with a camera was both spectacular and captivating. Her great grandmother just didn't take pictures. She created life. Her pictures looked more alive than the actual subject in the view finder. Her photographed faces didn't show lines, they depicted age and experience along with hidden emotions. Her lens unearthed those emotions exposing buried secrets. She captured epic sagas, each frame of film depicting artistic creativity framed with respect and painstaking dignity. She had the knack for catching on film what most eyes would never see. It was her great grandmother's form of magic. Some eyes, however, eyes that recognized special talents, also recognized Ellie van Sestern's form of magic. The stories that identified and elevated Ellie van Sestern into a world reserved for males exploded and she never looked back.

Stories about Emmy's great grandmother were documented with facts. She had been the first woman photographer ever to be allowed to cover the White House. That was near the end of World War II when Harry Truman was president. *Life* magazine liked Eleanor van Sestern's work with a camera so much that her pictures appeared in numerous issues back then; once there was even a cover shot.

Emmy didn't see a status magazine cover. She saw beauty on film. Articles about Ellie van Sestern became a part of Emmy's soul. "All of those famous people," she had said, her Brownie camera and the antique Rollieflex listening intently as they sat on the tiny shelf next to her bed. "Granna Ellie, you were one awesome lady." With those words, Emma Gracie Waveland elevated her great grandmother and placed her on a pedestal. Emma wanted to be just like her and was well on her way, according to her father, "of being just like that Shutter Bug."

Where most little girls saved their money in piggy banks, Emmy placed hers in two envelopes; one marked, *Cameras and Equipment* and the other, like the first, scribbled in pencil, the words, *Developing and Printing*.

His daughter's frugal habits humored Walt Waveland his telling his wife, "That kid of ours has a one track mind and is so tight fisted when it comes to saving money for her hobby she could squeeze a penny so hard Abe Lincoln would look like he was gasping for air."

Emmy and her Ellie, as she nicknamed her Rollieflex camera, had become inseparable. Her new digital camera now sat on the shelf besides her Kodak Brownie. The pictures she took with the Rollieflex amazed, sometimes even flabbergasted, her parents and family members. "All your Uncle Joe ever did when he took pictures," Emmy's Aunt Cecilia had complained, "was to show what kind of shoes people wore. You never saw their faces because he cut off their heads." Other relatives and friends chimed in. "Your Uncle Stan never takes picture of his kids or any other human beings," her Aunt Loretta carped. "He's enthralled with taking pictures of lakes. Doesn't matter what lake or where it's at, he takes pictures of water." The comparisons and complaints raged on but Emmy didn't care. What came into the viewfinder of her Ellie came into the viewfinders of millions of cameras. Emmy, however, saw her subject differently than what was seen in those other view-finders. There was a slight angle that others didn't see; a background that offered the unique. When others, including her Uncle Stan, saw only water, she saw an artistic ripple, a hypnotic swirl, a bubble bursting, a mysterious fin or a lazy, drifting leaf on its watery death bed. She saw a birth, a creation, a laboratory experiment succeeding beyond wildest expectations. One of her pictures humbled all of her Uncle Stan's collection of water scenes. Her Uncle Joe even sorted through his photographs depicting headless subjects wearing shoes and tossed them into the garbage.

Science and technology chased at Emmy's heels like a rabid dog. Emmy had one digital camera, but tempting advertise-ments showed cameras with detachable lenses and features she never dreamed possible. Her parents even bought her an iPhone. "It's for keeping you safe and to be used in case of emergency," her father had warned. "It ain't no toy."

"Your father's right," her mother quickly added. "You be careful. Your father and I don't want to see any of those Selfie pictures floating around."

Her mother's statement siding with her father confused Emmy. Her mother seldom sided with her father. However, Emmy could take all the pictures she wanted with her new iPhone and none of her human subjects would ever know. She giggled as she e-mailed those pictures to friends. She even took Selfies but hated how she looked. After several Selfies, she remarked to her Brownie and Ellie, "Geez, how stupid."

Emmy quickly discovered the world of the computerized photo shop. She could do in minutes what it took her hours to do in the tiny dark room her father had set up in part of a storeroom in the family basement. The click of a mouse replaced the mixing of developers and fixers. Thermometers, plastic trays, tongs and clamps were carefully stored in a box. Her father sold her enlarger. The computerized process of manipulating a photograph with a mouse click overpowered her in the beginning. Then she got the hang of it and that night before going to bed she prayed to her great grandmother thanking her for not trying to punish her for putting her Ellie on her bookshelf. "Ellie will always be in my heart and soul," she had said to her great grandmother before sliding under the sheets. The next morning at breakfast she was too nervous to eat. "Daddy," she had said on the verge of tears. "How can I ever thank you and Mommy for letting me do the one thing in life I really love?"

"You just did," her father said. He smiled and then shook

her to the core of her soul. "I just told your mother that our entire family is going to Florida this summer. I know it's hot and humid and very few people go to Florida in the summer." He smiled. "But I got a good deal and our hotel room is air conditioned."

"Did you say Disney World," she whispered.

Her father nodded, his eyes twinkling. "They even offer an African safari."

"We're going where this summer?" Emmy's oldest brother, Josh, asked. He sounded surprised, his surprise carrying an edge of displeasure. "But that's during summer baseball," he complained. "I can't miss that many games. The coach will bench me forever."

"Me too," said her next older brother, Scott, his cereal spoon hanging, milk spilling on his t-shirt.

"Me three," echoed Todd, her youngest brother. He had a striking resemblance to the character from "Mad" magazine and his spoon was dripping milk on his Bears sweatshirt.

A father looked at his three boys, the twinkle gone from his eyes. "Did I miss something?" he asked. There was a calmness in his voice that a brought a chill to the kitchen.

Five sets of eyes and ears waited.

"Did someone forget to tell me dat three scouts from the Major Leagues were here signing my teenage sons to six figure contracts?"

Five sets of eyes didn't blink. Their ears, however, heard every syllable.

Walt looked at Josh, Scott and Todd. Empathy, sympathy and understanding were not present on his face. "Mmmm," he muttered. "Now let me see if I understand your logic for not

wanting to go on a family vacation to Disney World." There
was another pause; this one longer and eerier. "Let me get this
straight. You three are concerned about being benched if you
miss a week to go on a family vacation." His pause technique to
emphasize a point was in high gear. The pause was also
accompanied by the lobes on his ears growing red as if an ugly
rash had attacked him. "The last time I looked, you three had
batting averages dat were slightly less dan what each one of you
weighs."

They could see the red spreading from their father's ears
across his cheeks and up to his forehead. This was, they knew
from experience, not a good sign.

"Well, guys," he said, the icy calmness still chilling the room.
"Your old man is going to give you a few pointers on how to
raise your batting averages." His forehead wrinkled as he
looked at each one of them.

Emmy and her mother were spared the look.

"What you guys need is to get your timing back; you're
going to need to see the ball better. You guys press too hard.
Maybe you need some extra time in the batting cage. Perhaps
you need to relax. In the major leagues, the teams all have
sports' psychologists when players get into a slump. Sometimes
managers even have their biggest stars ride da pines. You
know, sit on da bench." His eyes hadn't moved off the three
boys and their spoons were still dangling somewhere between
mouths and cereal bowls. "Now I've got da cure for what ails
you three." He paused before asking, "Do you know what dat
is?"

They knew.

Chapter 2

Emmy's mother, her head barely inside her daughter's bedroom door, asked, "Do you have everything organized for our trip to Disney World?" Her query was filled with a loving concern. "We leave tomorrow." There was a pause and she added. "You know what a stickler your father is about leaving on time. Once he starts the car...." She didn't finish her statement.

Emmy knew that if she forgot her head her father wouldn't turn back. "I know, Mom," she answered. "Daddy turns into a different person when he's trying to reach where he wants to go." Emmy knew that their trip to Disney World and an animal safari was done according to a complex plan based on many variables controlled almost entirely by her father. The one variable her father could not control was her mother's head snapping in the direction of her father and the cold glare that cut through the car like a James Bond 007 laser beam if he ignored her suggestion for a rest stop. When the seat belt was fastened across her father's chest with a click and he pointed the car in the direction of their destination her father tuned out everything except the cars around them and their drivers. All those steering other vehicles displeased him and he let them know through a series of muffled derogatory comments. Each comment was quickly followed by her mother using her husband's full name.

"Walter James Joseph," she would say, his middle and Confirmation names showing her displeasure at her husband's colorful, creative monikers at his fellow motorists. "There are tender ears riding in the back." At this point, Betty Waveland would pause to swallow her venom then state in a way too loving way. "Or, have you forgotten?"

Emmy and her brothers were always amazed at their father's linguistic creativity and how he managed to string together a sentence demonizing the driver of another car without, for the most part, repeating himself. Their father had his favorite descriptive expressions that he relied on more than others. Emmy's brothers used to keep a tally sheet in the back seat on long trips to see what negative word or expression was used the most. Now, as Emmy's mother stood totally in her room, the Shutter Bug said, "I'm all packed, Mom. "I even got my toothbrush."

As far as Emmy was concerned, she was packed. She had her iPhone, her fist digital camera, an Olympus Camedia she had gotten for her tenth birthday and her new pride and joy, a digital single lens reflex with an extra lens—a seventy five millimeter telephoto that expanded her creativity to levels she never imagined. Besides, her camera came with a name that fit her personality--Rebel. She had been tempted to pack her Ellie and the Brownie as well, but decided against it. She didn't know if the old film she had stored like a miser for such an occasion would hold up on a safari, even if the safari was in Orlando, Florida. Always prepared, she had extra batteries and several blank memory cards that had enough storage to run General Motors. Her black leather camera bag weighed about as much as she did. She had stuffed her clothing and personal items into a denim pastel blue duffle bag adorned with pictures of colorful tropical birds. The very first item she packed was her magic Cracker Jack prize with Mickey Mouse's silhouette etched on the back; that went into the pocket of the shorts her mother had ironed for her.

The trip to Florida started on time. There had been a minimum of yelling from her father, especially at her brothers, before leaving. "Get the lead out and move your little butts," he said gruffly. "We ain't got all day." That warning came about ten minutes before their scheduled time of departure.

Emmy chose to sit in the back seat of their SUV, the vehicle designed to seat seven provided the passengers all had backsides the size of Emmy's. Her father took great pride in maintaining his eight year old truck as he referred to it. The design and precise assembling of Emmy's Rollieflex camera couldn't rival Walt Waveland's performing maintenance on his truck. He washed and waxed it like a teenage boy getting ready to go to his high school prom. Walt Waveland invented the term, detailing for washing a car and went several steps beyond by taking out a gigantic carton of cotton swaps to reach into the tiny cracks and crevices of the truck. He had installed a GPS even though he was a walking World Atlas and the former geography champion of his eighth grade class. His enjoyment came from talking back to the computer generated voice using degrading, demeaning comments. Another amenity he added to the truck was a TV monitor in back so his children could watch movies during long vacation drives. According to him, "That'll keep 'em quiet so they won't ask to stop and pee every five miles," he had said to his wife more times than she cared to hear.

Emmy knew her father seldom surprised anyone in the family with his words and behavior. He had shocked her when he came up with the money for her SLR digital camera. She had saved every cent she could get her hands on including pennies she found on the sidewalk and any loose change that had slipped behind cushions on the sofa and living room chairs. Her money was placed in her envelopes, but the amount for a new camera was way short when she had a chance to buy the camera on sale. Short was by more than eighty percent, but her father got her in the car and drove her to the store where she walked out beaming and clutching her new pride and joy in her arms. Her father's surprises continued. For their upcoming vacation trip he purchased several DVDs of old movies. "If we're going on a safari, then we should be prepared to recognize the wildlife we'll see," he said, informing his passengers just before he pulled away from the house. Two of his purchases included "King Solomon's Mines" and the other, "Hatari" an old John Wayne movie about collecting wild animals for zoos. Emmy watched that movie three times during the long drive to Florida and was pleased that her brothers slept through the second and third showings. During those repeat showings she put together a list of wild animals she would photograph.

The trip went according to Walt Waveland's detailed travel plans. There was a gas stop when the gas gauge registered one quarter full. He had once prided himself on getting the warning light to flash before stopping to refuel. That exercise in male pride ended after he ran out of gas on a desolate stretch of road near the Wisconsin border and Michigan's Upper Peninsula when they were on their way to visit relatives. A five mile hike to find gas shifted pride into common sense; that and a cold stare from his wife that lasted the entire visit and part of the return trip home.

Walt Waveland always made one planned non-gas stop. That was to a Shoney's Big Boy, his favorite restaurant. His family thought the size of restaurant's sign was garish and lacked taste, but their father thought it was more than cool stating to his three sons, "If you guys ate like the kid in that sign, you wouldn't be worrying about sitting on the bench when we get back home." He paused and shook his head. "Now get in there and load up on the breakfast buffet. You three need some meat on your skinny bones." He paused again. "And dem dare is orders from headquarters."

They arrived in Orlando and Emmy's father followed the directions from his GPS to the hotel where they had reservations. Emmy thought that the pictures on the brochure had to be of another hotel. "Is this where we're staying, Daddy?" she asked politely without trying to indicate how disappointed she was that the dreary outside façade of the hotel looked nowhere like the sparkling gem depicted on the brochure.

"Dis must be da place," her father remarked, trying to be funny.

The other passengers didn't see the humor. Betty Waveland was too tired from the ride to act like 007 and her three sons saw a vacation from Hell looming in front of them. That didn't bother their father. He had, according to his proud statement, "Shaved forty-seven minutes off our ETA." Walt Waveland quickly transformed himself into a Marine Drill Instructor marching his troops to the check-in desk where they were greeted by a young clerk not much older than Josh. He flashed a bored smile and greeted the new arrivals with an equally bored, "Welcome to the gateway to the Magic Kingdom, folks. We at the Shady Palms hope you'll have an enjoyable stay with us."

Walt flashed the contents of an ecru colored envelop cluttered with pictures of Disney characters and signed a credit card slip. He smiled and returned to being Gunnery Sergeant Walt of *Semper Fi* fame and began barking out orders to his children. He knew better than to order his wife. Terse commands bordering on the harsh side had his children lining up in single file, luggage in hand and pointed in the direction of the elevator that would take them up to the top floor of the two story hotel.

"Wow," echoed across their hotel room that was more like a Presidential Suite. They all caught a glimpse of a large body of water visible way off in the distance through the sliding glass door leading to the balcony.

"Is that the Pacific Ocean?" Scott asked.

"That ain't the Pacific," replied Josh, appearing to share in his father's geography expertise. "That's the Gulf of Mexico."

"Really?" asked Todd.

"It's the Atlantic," their father said, his authoritative correction clearing any doubt from the room even though he was too tired from driving to care.

None of them knew they were looking at a corner of Bay Lake.

Walt Waveland felt a sense of satisfaction the moment he opened the door to their accommodations at the hotel and caught the look on his wife's face. He gave her a nod and she returned it with a slight nod of approval. Betty Waveland was pleased and all of his oceans, seas, gulfs and lakes were in line— whatever they were called and wherever they were located. He wasted no time in assigning bunks not beds. Since the sun was starting to set, he ordered everyone to get in bed. "I want to get an early start tomorrow morning to beat the crowds. They behave worse than the animals we'll see on our safari." Before his family realized, Walt Waveland was snoring, fully clothed on the living room sofa as if he were at home.

Emmy wasted no time in unpacking her camera bag. She ignored her duffel even with her mother's urging, "Put your things on hangars. You don't want to walk around looking like a laundry basket." She repeated her urging a half dozen times. Emmy nodded, muttered that she would and then continued checking her cameras to see if any damage had been caused during the trip. Any damage was unlikely since the camera bag sat on her lap the entire trip.

Satisfied that her cameras came out unscathed, Emmy caught a glimpse of the setting sun through the curtains of the balcony door in their room. She was amazed at the size of the balcony. There was a circular wrought iron ornate table painted in a lilac color with two matching padded chairs decorated with palm trees. Off to the side was an end table similar in color and design as the table and chairs. The size of the orange fireball disappearing in the west caught Emmy's eye and she dashed inside to grab the nearest camera she could. In a moment there were the faint sounds of a lens painting what an excited tiny artist's eyes captured.

Chapter 3

Emmy didn't sleep that night. After the sun had set and just as her mother was heading for her bedroom, she had promised her mother saying: "I'm right behind you, Mom." Then quickly she added, "And, I'll hang up my stuff just like you want. I won't look all wrinkled when we go on that safari tomorrow. I promise." Her vow lasted about as long as it took the sun to sink behind a horizon scattered with palm trees, satellite TV dishes sprouting from roof tops and a smattering of garish billboards. Emmy kept looking out in the direction where the sun had set hoping to see the Magic Kingdom. All the looking in the world wouldn't have brought Disney World into view. Their Shady Palms hotel suite was on the opposite side of the Magic Kingdom.

In minutes after her mother had closed the bedroom door, Emmy began to feel weary. The hours spent being cooped up in the back of the SUV for what seemed like an eternity had caught up to her. Ever the rebel, she challenged sleep. Her camera had not left her hands since the family arrived. She sat down on one of the balcony chairs and looked toward a quickly darkening west in hopes of discovering another subject to store on her memory card. There were none, at least none that appealed to her discriminating taste. Bored and her eyelids drooping, she went inside. She found her camera bag and pulled out her iPad.

She attached a small cable from her camera to the tiny lap top computer and began to transfer her sunset pictures to the Picasa program. Her intent was to do some experimenting with the various images of the sun she had photographed. Blurred vision accompanied by a chin that kept hitting her tiny chest, she followed the growing desire to find her bed and put her creative urges on hold. In a moment she curled up on fold-away cot off to the side of the living room. Earlier, she had said to her father, "I'm not sleeping in the same room with my brothers." Her rationale spilled out. "They're gross pigs." Emmy was soon sleeping as sound as her father but without the nocturnal noises he emitted.

Breakfast found the family standing on the balcony. Betty Waveland's plan, her husband concurring, was to have orange juice and multi-grain, multi flavored breakfast health bars jammed with granola. Eating would be an all day affair at Disney and Walt Waveland knew his three sons would put a substantial dent in the vacation budget on the first day and every day thereafter. "You guys should go on a real safari," their father had said to his sons. "Maybe you could shoot a lion or a hippo for lunch. That would be much cheaper than buying you hamburgers and all that other junk food you stuff down your gullets during the course of a day."

Betty Waveland had planned and allocated one breakfast bar each for her, her husband and daughter. The boys got two each.

She had bought enough bars for the week. By the time they left for the Magic Kingdom and their safari on the first day, there were three and a half bars left. The insulated cooler they had transported five half gallons of orange juice packed with ice cubes now stood keeping cool one solitary half gallon carton, that being half full.

Always the protective mother hen, Betty Waveland smeared an extra blob of sun block on each of her children's noses as they marched out of the hotel room toward the lobby. Emmy got the last blob, actually three, both of her ears getting the protective motherly treatment. She didn't care. The strap of her camera bag was slung over her shoulder and deep in the right hand pocket of her hiking shorts was her magical Cracker Jack prize giving off warmth that felt like she was going on an exciting adventure. The last thing on her mind was how hot the sun would get and sun block. After all, she had surmised, it would eventually set that evening and the night would be cool and relaxing just as it had been their first night in Florida. The prize in her pocket all but guaranteed that.

Chapter 4

Walt Waveland attempted to explain what all of them would be seeing when they went on their Magic Kingdom safari. His three sons didn't seem interested in those details, asking their father, "Do the Atlanta Braves really have their spring training at Disney?" Dozens of related questions were fired at their father, each one containing at least one sentence ending with the words, "we go?" Preceding the word, we were words such as *can*, *will* and *when will*.

Their father fielded each question as if he were a major league shortstop, making every attempt to calmly provide a satisfactory explanation. The questions soon challenged his vacation planning itinerary and a desire, according to Josh, "I don't want to go on some dumb safari when I can see major league ball players practicing. Boy, I bet I could learn all kinds of things about batting," he continued, appearing out of breath.

"Yes, you can," said a father to his first born. "Only you'll be learning from summer instruction league players and coaches," he continued. "Some day, if you ever get off the pines, you just might make a summer instructional camp."

Josh wanted his father to elaborate, but got the feeling he shouldn't.

Walt Waveland looked at his son and raised his right hand. "Do you know what dis is?"

Josh nodded and said a touch of cockiness in his voice. "Yeah, Dad, it's your hand." He smiled. "Even our spoiled little brat sister knows that."

His other brothers chuckled.

Their father did not.

Emmy didn't see the humor. The only time she saw humor in what any of her brothers did or said was when they got a stern talking to by their father. Secretly she wished they would experience her father's hand. They never did. "Wrong," she heard her father say to the answer about his right hand. She saw her father smile and then say, "It's a Louisville Slugger." She saw him point at her brother's head and heard his next question. "And, do ya know what dis is?"

Josh, as cocky as ever, gave a sarcastic smile. "Are you pointing at my head, Dad?"

"Nope," replied Josh's father. "I'm pointing at the other element needed to improve your batting average so ya won't have to sit on da bench all summer because you went with your family on a dumb safari to Disney World." He gave a casual glance at his right hand that was still extended. "Louisville Slugger," he repeated. Then he pointed at his son's head again. "Official major league baseball," he said, his smile now gone. "Do ya know what happens when a bat meets a ball?" he asked, not giving his son a chance to answer. "It means da two most beautiful words in the world." He looked at his three sons. "And since you three Rhodes Scholars ain't got a clue of what I'm talking about, dose two words are, 'Play ball'." He smiled. "And play ball means learning how to duck when da high fast one zeroes in on your batting helmet." His right hand did a slow twisting motion. "It's learning how to get up out of da dirt and get back in da batter's box. It's getting your batting average up so you won't have to be a bench warmer when you get back home." His father's eyes traveled to his other two sons who weren't smiling any more.

Walt Waveland, his right hand still up, raised his left hand. He glanced at his right hand and said, "Louisville?" Then he looked at his left hand. "Or going on a safari to Africa?" His look turned way too serious for everyone in view. "Do you three aspiring Appalachian League all-stars know how long it would take a baseball to drop from the top of Mt. Kilimanjaro to the ground and land on an imaginary batting helmet?" There was a faint smile. "The batting helmet would be sitting atop your empty head." He stopped and looked puzzle, then started again. "Your old man is sure a stupid guy, don't ya know. I only counted one empty head." His eyes bounced from one son to the next. "I'm gonna need two more batting helmets and two more balls to take care of the two extra empty heads, heh."

Emmy knew her father's bark was greater than his bite. She didn't think he had a bite, at least one she never experienced. Her brothers weren't about to find out. Then, again, neither was Emmy. She had heard her father explain to her brothers once about respect for their mother. "If I ever hear one of you direct a word at your mother that begins with the sixth letter of the alphabet, you'll find out what it'll be like to catch a double header without wearing equipment." He paused then added,

"And, dat also means without wearing a protective cup."

Emmy knew exactly what her father meant. Growing up with three older brothers provided her with a liberal education. She remembered her father's litany of warnings to her brothers, each warning indicating that the culprit, according to him, would play every game of baseball under the grass and not on top of it. Emmy recalled how her father once looked at her during one of his rare warnings when her brothers weren't around and said, "And, young lady, that includes you. You can't take pictures when you and your camera lens are under da grass."

The next day her father paid for her new SLR camera.

Emmy was the first in their van, her camera bag held in a near death grip on her lap. Her brothers quickly piled in the car analyzing their father's analogy of a Louisville Slugger coming in contact with their heads. They knew that would never happen in a million life times, but there was also the element of doubt even though so miniscule.

"Everyone ready for da first day of our dumb vacation to Disney and all of those dumber theme parks?" Walt Waveland asked, the engine turning over with a perfectly tuned purr.

A series of grunts came from the back seats.

"Did you children know that there are many different parks that make up Disney World," their mother asked her voice cheerful.

More grunts came from the back seat, these from her three sons.

"There are the Magic Kingdom, Epcot, Hollywood Studios and the Animal Kingdom where we're going on safari," Emmy blurted out.

Three heads turned around, eyes glaring at her.

Emmy surged on. "I checked that out on Google before we left," she said, feeling good that she had put her brothers in their place. "There's also the Sports Complex where that major league baseball team practices and some water parks; fireworks at night too."

Emmy's father hid his smile. Her mother couldn't. "Good job, Emma," she said. Her head turned slightly. "Now aren't you three boys ashamed of yourselves for pouting about going on safari?"

The three boys wanted to put a muzzle on their baby sister.

"You boys have no idea what your father has planned for you," Betty Waveland said. "And, that includes you, Miss Shutter Bug."

Everyone in the car knew something was wrong when Walt Waveland started questioning his GPS. The questions always showed up when he ignored the computerized directions and talking back to the voice that kept telling him to turn around. After a continuous heated exchange and appearing miles from their destination, he pulled into a gas station that had one lonely gas pump standing in front of a small frame building with peeling paint and a screen door with a hole torn into it around the handle.

The passengers watched the driver shuffle toward the store mumbling with every step. What seemed like an eternity later in the growing warmth of the Florida sun, Walt Waveland returned. He was laughing. The laughing continued as he pulled out of the gas station and handed a paper bag into the back seat. "Jerky," he said, his laugh starting up again. After retracing his route for over a half hour and not quite apologizing to the voice on his GPS, he looked at his wife and then into the rearview mirror. "Do any of you know what a missing link is?" he asked.

Three mouths stuffed with dried meat said nothing. Emmy swallowed and then asked, "Does that have something to do with evolution, Daddy?"

Her brothers groaned.

"Well, Emmy, Charles Darwin was right on the money," he said. "That guy back at the store was an insult to the ape population of the world."

"Walt," interrupted Betty Waveland. "It's not nice to be critical of our fellow human beings," she said. "We are all God's children."

"I'm not being critical my pet," he said trying not to laugh. "It's just dat dis guy kind of missed God's message." There was a silence in the car. "With that guy, when God gave out brains, he thought he said trains and he got to the station late and missed his."

"Oh, Walt."

Chapter 5

The passengers in the van soon discovered that they were on more than the advertised Kilimanjaro Safari. They had gone from one van to another one. This van was open air with a canvas top and designed for sightseeing. The body of the too long open vehicle was painted in a camouflage style and had what appeared to be rations of water, food and emergency gear lashed to the top and back in assorted wooden crates. There was also dented container also in camouflage paint that was a gasoline can. There were ten rows of benches that offered unhindered views of the African scenery.

Emmy was quick to slide to one side of what her father described as an overgrown Land Rover. She didn't want anything or anyone blocking her view, especially the view from her SLR. Her camera was ready in seconds and so was her magical Cracker Jack good luck charm still sending her a sense of adventure from the pocket in her hiking shorts.

The sightseeing truck began to creep forward, the driver beginning his narration as if it were recorded. His name was Jean Claude and he was dressed and looked like he had been raised in Tanzania and had explored the country from Mount Kilimanjaro across the Serengeti to watch the Wildebeest migration across the plains and swollen crocodile filled rivers. Emmy understood everything he said having devoured every word that Wikipedia flashed up on her computer screen before the family had left for Orlando. She knew that Tanzania had once been called Tanganyika the country's name having been changed as the Dark Continent was going through a long overdue period of decolonization in the early 1960's. The transition had been one that was not pleasurable to the colonizers and those who wanted their independence. Blood had been shed on both sides, but that was something the Disney folks didn't want to elaborate on. Emmy wasn't that interested in history either. Her two digital cameras were at the ready and the ride didn't disappoint her. She couldn't click her shutters fast enough. Had she been using real 35 millimeter film instead of a digital memory card, her parents would have had to take out a second mortgage on their house to finance her hobby which had now turned into a mania.

The camouflaged customized touring vehicle was loaded to capacity and crept along a rut road that had animals on both sides taking their own sweet time roving with it. Emmy was glad she had her telephoto lens. The animals appeared right in her face almost touching her nose. At times she thought she could smell the elephants. Other times she thought she could even feel the heat of what appeared to be an agitated hippo on her face. She was ecstatic. Everyone on the safari was ecstatic. That's what the Disney organization engineers had designed and wanted, and that's what they and their elated customers were getting. It was a happy, exciting, informative adventure and the Land Rover, The Rover as Walt Waveland now called it, spilled out smiling faces like baseball fans clamoring to enter their favorite ballpark on Opening Day. Then Mother Nature turned extremely bad natured for no apparent forecasted reason. In less than an instant, the sunny Florida sky molted into a grotesque black. Streaks of lightning did an eerie dance the bolts looking like they were aimed at the safari.

"Part of the show," Walt Waveland said to his wife over the increasing wind. "Disney thinks of everything to give the customers their money's worth."

The winds were now roaring and no one could hear Jean Claude, the driver, instruct the passengers to be calm. "It's only a passing thunder storm," he said into the tiny mouth piece of the microphone hung from his ear. No one heard him. Suddenly a vicious black cloud in the shape of a giant black rhinoceros charged at the Land Rover. It was bigger than an old fashioned steam locomotive. The cloud, however, was faster than the locomotive and looked like it could, indeed, leap tall buildings or anything else that got in its path. The roaring wind hit the Land Rover broadside with a vengeance. The canvas top was blown loose from the mounting slats and flapped helplessly for about three seconds before it was torn free and disappeared. Screams came from the Land Rover but those were only heard by the person screaming. The wind became a supersonic battering ram. Emmy could see Jean Claude wrestling to keep the vehicle from going on its side and sliding into the stream that ran alongside the road. He couldn't. Emmy felt the vehicle being lifted up and then rotating on its side. Before she realized, she saw her feet above her head. The vehicle was on its top. It didn't stay that way. Emmy saw her feet on the floor and then saw them again looking down at her. Thunder exploded and Emmy thought she lost her hearing as lightning joined the battering, crashing down around them. Emmy felt her mother grab her arm as the Land Rover made one final violent revolution before coming to a rest upside down in the stream.

Emmy had no idea that Jean Claude had activated the emergency features of the safari ride instantly. He would have his passengers to safety in a minute. Emmy never saw the windblown debris in the form of tree limbs and vegetation from the ground hurled at the Land Rover at what seemed like supersonic speeds only seen in Hollywood disaster films. Part of that debris smashed into the driver's side of the Land Rover. Emmy did see Jean Claude's arms and hands go up and then he disappeared from her sight. She had felt her mother's grip tighten and could see her lips moving but the howling winds swallowed up her words before tearing her loose from Emmy and picking her up and blowing her out of sight as if swallowed up by a tornado. Emmy saw, but couldn't hear the cries from the frightened passengers who were being tossed about in their seats like rag dolls.

The only thing Emmy hung on to was her camera bag, her arms wrapped around it in a death grip as she was jostled about like an out of control ping pong ball. Somehow, just before the truck had started its roll down hill, she managed to slide her camera into her shoulder bag. What totally amazed her was that she wasn't in a state of panic like the others. She was frightened, but somehow knew she would be protected from danger. Protection didn't come from her parents or her brothers or any nearby concerned passenger or even their driver Jean Claude. The entire time since the storm hit she could feel her good luck Cracker Jack charm protecting her. It was as if Mickey Mouse himself had wrapped his loving arms around her, whispering in her ear, "Believe, Emmy. Believe."

She could hear the whispered words distinctly. Then it was all she heard. The Land Rover was upside down and water was running through it. Emmy didn't know that she had been sucked out of the vehicle and was lying half in and half out of the water. She had the feeling that she was in the bathtub back home in the family house. She could see her mother kneeling alongside the tub holding a wash cloth foaming with giant soap bubbles. She had never seen bubbles that big. The bubbles rolled off the wash cloth and began popping in her face tickling her at first, then growing in size and strength. Then the popping stopped and the bubbles, flexing their new muscles, began to pummel her. She tried to raise her arms to protect herself from the pain, but couldn't. They appeared to be tied. She glanced down and thought she could see the strap from her camera bag wrapped around her. She froze. It wasn't her camera strap but a giant snake was coiled around her, slowly constricting, squeezing, and taking her breath away. "Granna Ellie," she screamed. "Help me. Help me!" Then her world turned blacker than the unexpected storm that had smashed into the African safari adventure.

Emmy felt herself floating on a puffy, white cloud. Was she dreaming or was it what her father had told her about Disney World making dreams come true? "All you have to do is believe and try hard enough," her father had said, "and you'll see your dreams happen."

Confusion joined Emmy on her cloud. So did two giant stuffed animals in the shape of baby elephants. The elephants were pink in color and she tried to wrap her arms around the elephants' trunks, but the animals nudged her away. "Gee," she said to the pair, "I only want to give you a hug." The elephants slowly vanished. Her curious brain began to generate questions that didn't seem to have logical answers. "Puffy white cloud?" she asked. "Giant stuffed pink elephants with trunks that kept pushing me away? Why?" Then she felt a flash of panic. "My Ellie!" she shouted out. "Where's my Rebel!" She was tossing and turning on her cloud, her arms flailing at it, punching holes in the cotton ball like vapor, spreading it apart, bringing other images into view as if looking out the side opening of the Land Rover into a dissipating silken mist. She saw the shadow of a person coming toward her vanishing cloud. "Granna Ellie," she called out. "Is that you? Is it really you?" The figure came closer. "Help me, Granna Ellie," she pleaded. "I'm scared."

"Easy, Missy," a voice said to her in a strange accent.

Emmy could see bright colors adorning the voice. "Granna Ellie is that really you?" she asked again. "Oh, how I've always wanted to meet you, to talk to you, to get to know you." Emmy felt tears streaming down her cheeks. She was wet and shivering. "You're my idol, Granna Ellie." Then Emmy heard the words again.

"Easy, Missy," said the voice more comforting than her own mother's voice.

Emmy felt herself falling through a giant hole that had ripped open in her cloud. Instinctively, her arms went around her camera bag to protect her equipment. She didn't fear for herself. "No, no, no," she yelled out. "You're not going to get my Ellie. I won't let you." Her arms squeezed her camera bag harder and she buried her face into the black leather. She recoiled. The bag felt wet and slippery as if covered in slime. "My Rebel," she said her voice almost in a shout.

"Oh, poor *ting*," the soothing accented voice said.

Emmy wanted to reach out and latch on to the thick, soothing accent surrounded by bright colors but her arms wouldn't let go of her bag. She felt pressure under each arm and then a sensation of being pulled through the slime she had felt early until her body was resting on a warm grassy comforter. Her arms clutched her camera bag even tighter as she began to toss and turn.

"My you frisky," the voice said, laughter joining the accent. "So much energy after riding rapids." A bright light pierced Emmy's closed eyes. It hurt her. Emmy wanted to rub at her eyes but she wouldn't let go of her camera bag. "Make it go away," she murmured. "Make it stop hurting." She tried to roll from side to side, but that too brought on pain. "I'm not going to let my brothers see me like this," she said, her statement sounding strong and tough. "No way."

Dare others?" the accented voice asked.

Emmy bolted up right and managed to say, "My family." Then she looked into the face of a woman surrounded in colors. The face was black. Big brown eyes loving and caring warmed her. Emmy could see she wore what looked like a small turban a blinding white in color. "You're not Granna Ellie."

The woman let out a jovial laugh. "Me Bickie," she said.

Emmy's look was filled with questions. She felt the woman's hand on her forehead.

"You hurt here?"

Emmy didn't waste a second. "I don't know," she said. "I don't know where I'm at or who you are."

"Me Bickie," said the woman repeating her name. A friendly smile filled her round face. Her lips parted exposing a mouth full of perfect white teeth that was accentuated by two gold upper teeth sparkling proudly from the middle. "I cook for Mister Mar and his men. They call me Bickie because I make dem da best biscuits dey ever does eat."

Emmy listened and continued to cling on to the warmth of Bickie's smile. She latched on to every word. Suddenly she felt afraid and wanted to be with her family. She didn't want to be on a safari, didn't want to take pictures of animals and didn't want to be in what looked like a jungle along the bank of a wide river. She wanted to fight with her brothers. She wanted to be with her family, giving them hugs and telling them how much she loved them. Her eyes began to well up with tears and she could feel her arms unloosen enough so that her camera bag dropped into her lap. Cautiously she asked, "Where am I?"

"You in Tanganyika, Missy," said Bickie her accent warm and soothing. "You in Africa." Her statement was joined by her dark brown face answering Emmy's question.

"Africa?" repeated Emmy. "In the Africa located in the Animal Kingdom at Disney World?" she asked, appearing out of breath

Bickie smiled. "Don't know Dizzy Whirl," she said, while continuing to smile. "I know Serengeti, Maasai, Kilimanjaro and Mister Mar. I know crew. I know getting animals for zoos." She paused. "Mar a good man. Mister Howdy, Mister Bomba, Jean Claude and da others, dey good too," she said.

"Jean Claude," Emmy repeated in a screech. "He's here?"

"You know Mister Jean Claude, Missy?"

"I don't really know him," Emmy began to explain, an excitement in her voice that caused Bickie concern. "But he was driving our Land Rover when the storm came up and then I didn't know what happened until I saw you, Bickie. It is okay if I call you, Bickie?"

Bickie broke into a grin. "You better call me Bickie or dey be none my homemade biscuits for you when we get back to da compound."

"Compound?" asked Emmy, her head not hurting as much, and the pain she had been feeling throughout her body seeming to be gone. She felt herself warming up to the loving jovial black woman named Bickie. She also felt a warm sensation in the pocket of her hiking shorts and knew her magical good luck charm with the etching of Mickey Mouse's head was causing the warmth. She knew that nothing could harm her now.

Emmy walked alongside of Bickie and noticed it right away. "Bickie," she said cautiously, "what happened to your foot?"

Bickie didn't break her stride, a walk with a limp and a loping gate. "Crocodile, Missy."

"Crocodile?" asked Emmy in a whisper coated in admiration and fear. She had never seen anyone with half a foot let alone walk alongside of one on a path somewhere in Africa. Emmy was in awe of this woman who had a sandal glad right foot and only half a foot strapped onto the other sandal that looked like it had been trimmed down to fit the partial left foot.

"Me not see, Missy," said Bickie. "Me tinking bout birthday dinner for Miss Ellie."

"Miss Ellie?" asked Emmy politely.

Bickie smiled at Emmy. "Miss Ellie take picture for zoo."

"Miss Ellie's here?" asked Emmy not sure whether to believe the woman or not.

"She here," said Bickie without taking her eyes off Emmy and the path they were walking. "I no remember how close my vegetable garden to river bank." She grinned. "Crocodile he jump. Me jump too. Save half a foot." She let out a chuckle. "But save Bickie."

"Bickie," Emmy started. She gave a nervous pause. "Did you say Miss Ellie?"

"Dat I do, Missy," said Bickie. "She be da crew's picture taker. "Dat dare zoo company wants pictures of all da animals Mister Mar and his crew round up. Miss Ellie, she works for the zoo company. So do Miss Schnapps." Bickie stopped and grinned when she saw the quizzical look Emmy gave her. "Miss Schnapps no real name, continued Bickie. "Da crew give dat when she celebrate too much at her birthday. She Annemarie. She daktari for animals who get sick. She heal me. She look out after crew." She paused. "Medicine man no like Annemarie. He put curse on her. She bad medicine."

"Bickie, could you tell me more about this Miss Ellie?" Emmy asked politely as if she never heard a word Bickie had said to her. She continued to walk along the path with her new friend without realizing she may have needed the services of this Annemarie person. Knowing there was someone called a medicine man in the area didn't make her comfort level go up. She had seen too many old movies on television that painted a clear picture stating that all medicine men were evil.

"If you listen, Bickie tell once about Miss Ellie. Her da picture taking lady," replied Bickie. "She very nice. So all folk on Mister Mar's crew." She smiled at Emmy. "I tink you like Mister Tab and Mister Buster. Dey fun. They have dangerous jobs. Most dangerous for da zoo. Maybe dat's why day are always play joke on people." Bickie smiled. "Dose two make Mister Mar crazy in da head."

As the path curved to the right away from the river, the jungle appeared to thin out. Emmy could see what looked like a group of one story buildings, some frame, others made out of what appeared to be branches of trees. Emmy kept up her pace with Bickie and for the first time noticed that the woman was carrying what appeared to be a bulging burlap sack. "Bickie," Emmy asked, again trying to be polite; not a pest like her father had instructed in their car on the drive to Florida. "What are you carrying in the bag?"

"Bickie carry dinner," she said, without any show of an expression. She looked at Emmy and gave her a broad smile, her two gold front teeth glistening in the sun. "My garden near where I find you. Best place for me grow *mchicha*."

Emmy didn't have to ask.

Bickie continued to smile. "Mister Mar say mchicha like American spinach," explained Bickie. "He and crew dey all like Bickie's mchicha and her corn and beans. Dat called makande."

"Does Miss Ellie like your mchicha and makande," Emmy asked.

"Oh, Missy," Bickie chuckled. "You almost funny as Mister

Tab and Mister Buster. Miss Ellie, I tink, she gonna like you."

Emmy could see a heavy wire fence circling what had to be the compound. Circling the building was a second heavy wire fence with a gate inside joining the two areas and several other gates, two large ones allowing access to a huge area where she could see several monstrous animals standing, unconcerned with the world around them. "Is that the compound, Bickie?"

"Dat is, Missy. Dat be your new home until Mister Mar find out where you from and get you back dar."

"I can tell him where I live," replied Emmy, feeling somewhat disappointed that she wouldn't have a chance to stay. She could see so many pictures taking shape in her mind. This was better than Disney World and her safari. She looked out past the compound and could see only a vast grassy plain punctuated with a rare, strange looking tree every so often. The plain was sprinkled with black moving dots way off in the distance. "What are those moving specks way out there?" she asked, still being polite.

"Africa's soul," stated Bickie as she led Emmy through a small wire gate that took them into the compound. "Dose black dots animals." She kept walking, leading Emmy to a large enclosed frame building with a thatched roof. "The Maasai treat dem with great respect. No killing. No eating."

Before she realized she was inside a large office facing a man who was standing by a long, wooden desk that appeared to have been made from thick tree trunks split into wide planks. The man was pointing to a large rolled out piece of paper on the desk and talking to several other men. He was taller than her father and much more muscular. He was also the handsomest adult man she had ever seen in person and thought he could be a movie star. She had all she could do to keep from reaching into her camera bag, taking out her Rebel and starting to snap as many pictures as she could. Her interest quickly changed to the furnishings in the room. Two large sofas and several stuffed chairs exactly like the chair her father used in their living room were covered with different animal hides. She recognized the zebra immediately and the pattern of a leopard. She had never seen a room like this in her life.

"Mister Mar," said Bickie without excusing herself for interrupting his conversation. "I find dis Missy on river bank by garden."

"Well now," said Mister Mar in a deep baritone voice that was minus the muscle of the rest of him. "And where'd you come from?"

Emmy tried to be polite as she explained every detail of the family trip to Disney World. She didn't know why she included Shoney's Big Boy. She told this man named Mister Mar about her brothers' fears of being benched—"My father called it riding the pines"—and driving on safari with their driver Jean Claude.

"Whoa now, Missy," said Mister Mar, his eyebrows going up with the name of one of his crew. "Jean Claude," he said, with a glance toward the men standing at the table. "Did you ever drive this young lady on any safari?"

The man addressed as Jean Claude turned and looked at Emmy.

Emmy's heart almost stopped. The man looked just like the Land Rover driver of the truck that turned over during the surprise storm. He was even wearing the same bush hat.

"No, sir, Mister Mar," said Jean Claude, his French accent very pronounced. "I'd of remembered driving around such a pretty young lady.

Emmy's faced burst into flames.

Laughter trickled out from the people in the room.

Bickie put a comforting arm around Emmy and tried to scowl at the others in the room but her eyes couldn't conceal her humor. "I find dis pretty missy half in and half out of da river by mchicha garden. She look like river took her far. She very lucky; so many rocks and animals and dose bad crocodiles in dat river. Yes, Missy, you be lucky."

Emmy could feel her good luck Cracker Jack sailor boy with Mickey Mouse's silhouette engraved across his back warm her.

Mister Mar cleared his throat and raised his eyebrows. "I never heard of a Disney World," he said. "Maybe you meant Disney Land, Missy." He looked at his male companions and then at Bickie. "Disney Land is kind of a new amusement park in California. Is that where you came from, Missy?"

Emmy didn't waste a second. "Oh, no, Mister Mar, my mommy and daddy drove me and my brothers to Disney World in Orlando, Florida. That's where I saw Mister Jean Claude. He was driving our Land Rover on our safari into the Serengeti when this big old storm came out of nowhere and tipped us over. The next thing I remembered is waking up and being pulled up that muddy bank of the river by Bickie.

Mister Mar looked at her, his eyes questioning as he sized up the situation. "Mmmm," he muttered, his eyes traveling to her camera bag. "And what's in your shoulder bag?" he asked politely, the others in the room paying attention. "If you grip that bag any harder, you might break what's in it."

Emmy continued to blush. "Oh, I'd never break my Ellie and my Rebel," she said, giving her shoulder bag a gentle pat. "And I'd never harm my iPhone either." She paused and gave Mister Mar a look that was almost pleading. "Mister Mar, do you think it would be okay if I could call my parents and let them know I'm safe?"

"Mmmm," muttered Mister Mar, "I don't think our short wave radio could reach Florida."

"My iPhone can," said Emmy, her free hand sliding the camera bag strap from her shoulder. She carefully set the bag down on the dusty wooden floor of the big office and unzipped it. In a moment she was holding up her iPhone with the leopard skin designed protective case. "See," she said.

The others in the room all circled around Emmy, their attention focused on the phone.

Emmy's finger pressed the on key and her phone came to life.

Mister Mar, Bickie and the others got closer to the phone in Emmy's hand.

Emmy looked frustrated and gave her iPhone a gentle shake. "Come on, bars where are you guys at?" She gave the phone another gentle shake. "I don't know what's wrong," she said, sounding as if she were about to start crying. "I can't get a signal. I don't even have one lousy bar." She looked at Mister Mar. "How far away is the nearest cellular phone tower?" she asked, not giving him a chance to answer. "Do you have A.T.&T, Verizon or who?" Her impatience was beginning to show, her frustration level building.

"Missy, I wouldn't know," he replied. He looked at the others in the room. "Do you folks know about any cellular phone towers in these here parts?" He smiled. "Do you think the Maasai might have built one on Kilimanjaro?"

The room filled with laughter.

A flash of light exploded in the room startling everyone including Emmy.

"Darn," blurted out Emmy. "I accidentally took your picture," she said, her right hand holding up the camera screen showing the curious faces clustered around Emmy.

"Dat's me," said a flabbergasted Bickie.

"How'd you do that?" asked the man known as Mister Howdy. He resembled the puppet from the old Howdy Doody children's television show complete with red hair, freckles and chubby cheeks.

"May I?" asked Mister Mar as he held his hand out toward Emmy. He carefully took the iPhone and examined the picture. "Is this the latest version of that Polaroid camera?" he asked looking impressed. "Very clever," he continued. "I bet Miss Ellie will really like to get her hands on this."

The others in the room smiled.

"Oh, this isn't a Polaroid camera," Emmy said. "There's no film. The picture is digital."

All of the faces in the room looked puzzled.

Emmy looked at her iPhone and noticed that it was in need of a charge. Her hand went into the camera bag for her charge cable and that's when she broke into tears.

Bickie was at her side in an instant. "No cry, Missy," she said, a comfort in her voice that didn't stop the flow of tears but did get Emmy to put her arms around Bickie's ample waist. Well, at least half way around.

Mister Mar returned Emmy's phone and gave a shrug, deep lines forming across his forehead. "Missy," he said, surprisingly soft for a rugged looking muscular man. "I promise you that we'll try to contact your parents." He rested his large hand gently on top of her head. "Before we do, you go with Bickie and she can get you set up with a place to sleep tonight. Okay?"

Emmy sniffled, removed her arms from around Bickie and quickly wrapped them as far as she could around Mister Mar's waist. "Thank you," she sniffled.

Mister Mar gave Emmy's head several gentle pats and said: "Now you go with Bickie and get settled in. Then you can help her in the kitchen to get dinner ready."

Chapter 6

Emmy saw Bickie give her a smile and nod her head in the direction toward the kitchen.

"Come, Missy," said Bickie in a mother's reassuring voice.

Emmy latched onto Bickie's calloused hand. She was so excited with her new surroundings and this group of adults who lived and worked on a real safari she wanted to grab her camera and start taking everyone's picture. She wasn't in Disney World now. This was Africa.

Her excitement quickly vanished as she entered the kitchen and saw two girls standing at a counter in the center of the kitchen. They were a little older than Emmy, gangly and taller, black and dressed identical in colorful red. The girls wore what looked like to Emmy shoulder to almost floor length sarongs.

The two black girls working with Bickie acted almost frightened when they saw Emmy. Their eyes were downcast and they didn't look up from their jobs which appeared to be getting the place settings ready for dinner. "They Maasai," said Bickie. She nodded in the direction of the girls who still didn't acknowledge Emmy's presence. "Dis Namunyak," said Bickie nodding at the first girl. "And dis blushing one here is Nalangu."

"Hi," replied Emmy sticking out her hand to shake theirs.

Both girls blushed and stepped back. Their eyes avoided Emmy's, their concentration appearing to be focused on the tasks they were performing.

"Hi," said Emmy again. "I'm Emmy." Her right hand was still extended.

Bickie laughed and took Namunyak by the hand and led her to Emmy. She then took the girl's hand and placed it in Emmy's. "Oh, Luck," she said using the girl's English translated name. "You shake hands. Mister Mar teach you dat."

Emmy looked at Bickie and then at the girl. "Hi, Luck," she said then repeated her greeting, "I'm Emmy."

Bickie smiled. "Her name, Namunyak means Lucky One." Bickie said, wiping her hands on a faded white apron wrapped around her. "She luckier dan me; jump longer and run faster dan me from crocodile who wanted her for dinner."

Emmy felt the girl's hand squeeze her hand and was surprised at the strength. She smiled at her new friend and looked at Bickie. "Really?" she asked. "Another crocodile?"

Bickie smiled. "Crocodiles love be by Bickie's garden," said Bickie her smile not wavering. Then Bickie took the other girl by the hand and placed it in Emmy's. "Emmy, dis Nalangu," said Bickie, watching the two girls shake hands. Nalangu blushed and Emmy emitted her own impish grin. "Da crew call her, Far," explained Bickie. "She come far away. Look like dead. Walked far away cross plains. Her people Maasai. Don't know why she leave. Could be she outcast."

"Really?" asked Emmy again as she squeezed Far's hand, smiled at her and said, "Hi, Far, I'm Emmy."

Far's eyes stayed downcast like those of Luck's who whispered something to her. She quickly looked up, smiled and

Emmy again was quickly taken back by the strength in her hand shake. Then her eye contact was gone, swapped for something of interest on the floor.

Emmy tried to make eye contact with Far by playfully squatting down and looking up into the Maasai teenager's eyes.

Far got flustered and turned away, nervous laughter echoing from her.

"She like you," said Bickie shaking her head at the girl's shy behavior. "Dey boat like you," said Bickie with a shrug. She glanced at the two Maasai girls then nodded at the kitchen counter where they had been preparing dinner. Bickie said something to the girls that Emmy didn't understand and they both resumed their jobs.

Bickie noticed Emmy's inquisitiveness immediately and said to her: "I speak Maa to girls. Dat Maasai language," she said, a grin showing her two glistening gold front teeth. "Later me teach *eeyu*," she continued pointing at Emmy.

"Me?" asked Emmy, showing the curios excitement of a twelve year old.

Bickie pointed her index finger at Emmy again. "See, you, eeyu, learn."

Emmy turned her attention to where Luck and Far were working. She noticed at once that both girls were almost bald. Emmy thought that her father had more hair on his face before he shaved in the morning. Both girls looked as if they might have five o'clock shadows on their heads. She also got a glimpse of their large pretty, penetrating eyes before they went into hiding. Emmy saw that the girls wore flimsy leather sandals and that they had several strands of colorful beads around their necks. "Your dresses are very pretty," said Emmy, discovering that she wanted to be friends with the girls.

Far and Luck knew Emmy was watching them. Neither looked up but started to giggle again as they continued with their chores.

"Dresses called *shukas*," said Bickie. "All Maasai wear."

"They're really cool," said Emmy, her exuberance for her strange, new exiting surroundings and friends growing. "I wish I had one."

Both Maasai girls looked up for a second and smiled at Emmy. They didn't understand a word she had said.

Bickie said something to Far and Luck in their Maasai tongue. Emmy wished she could understand the language, not knowing, not understanding, frustrated her. English was all she knew and all she had ever heard at home except when her father would get angry at her brothers. Then he unearthed words in German, Polish and Italian that Emmy knew were not her father's way of paying her brothers compliments.

"Come, Missy," said Bickie. "Show you room."

"Nice meeting you," said Emmy to the two girls as she followed Bickie. Her excitement and curiosity gave her the feeling that her feet were not touching the floor. Then she almost dropped to her knees when Bickie opened the door to her room. It looked like an oversized closet. Emmy looked up in silence at Bickie, her eyes asking what her tongue couldn't formulate.

"You sleep here," she said. Then she reached across to the far wall and pulled on what looked like a leather handle in the shape of a loop. Like magic, a single bed emerged from the wall, the foot of the bed stopping an inch from the doorway.

Emmy didn't know what to say.

"Mister Mar, he call dis a Murphy bed."

Emmy still didn't know what to say. She saw two tiny end tables, one in each corner, the tables butting up against the stained lumpy mattress. On top of one table were two folded sheets and a pillowcase. They sat neatly on a lumpy pillow covered with a variety of stains. The other table had several black plastic trays and what Emmy recognized immediately as a black cylindrical container that was used to develop film. There was a dark colored light bulb in the center of the ceiling with a long white pull string hanging down.

Bickie gave the string a yank and the bare bulb gave off a faint red glow. "Miss Ellie use room for zoo pictures."

Emmy felt her stomach spin out of control. "This is Miss Ellie's dark room?"

Bickie laughed at her statement. "Room red dark," said Bickie, her laughter trailing off. "Red light only work when generator work," she said as she pulled on the string and the light went off. "Electric off at midnight," she said in a business tone, her laughter gone. "You do everything before dat happen." Her look matched her tone. "No get up at night in Serengeti," she said, her head going back and forth. "Bad."

The single word of warning smothered Emmy's spinning stomach knocking away her excitement of being in the same room that her Granna Ellie used. The warning only bothered Emmy for an instant. Then Bickie had her by the hand and said, *"Maape."* Then she started leading her back to the kitchen. "You help Maasai friends, she said. "Bickie no do all."

Emmy didn't see the loving smile that accompanied the order.

The compound's dining room was in between Mister Mar's office and the kitchen. Like the office the dining room was large and rustic, the décor direct from Africa and the Serengeti. Unlike the office, the dining room consisted of a long wooden table with benches attached to the legs. When Emmy first saw the large table it reminded her of the tables in the Forest Preserves near Chicago where her family would sometimes go on picnics. There was a separate high back wooden chair at each end of the table, the table big enough to seat a dozen people. A large intriguing light fixture made of antlers hung from the ceiling. Three small, plain clay jars divided the table into thirds and each sported a bouquet of bright yellow flowers that brought both warmth and cheer to the room.

During dinner Mister Mar sat at the head of the table and Bickie at the other end. Bickie's end was closest to the kitchen and made it easier for her to go back and forth to the kitchen to get what was needed for the meal being served. Luck and Far were also waitresses but ate in the kitchen and then waited for a signal from Bickie to enter the dining room for instructions or to serve whatever needed to be served. Their signal was a tiny brass bell that Bickie rang with gusto. The words, *Coney Island* were inscribed on both sides of the bell.

Emmy sat in awe next to Bickie at the end of the table. Across from her sat Ellie. Emmy was too afraid to speak or eat. As the meal progressed, she saw Bickie give a faint nod in her direction and felt the woman's finger gently poke her in the side. "You eat," she heard her whisper.

Emmy picked up her fork and gave it a gentle poke into what looked like spinach.

"Mchicha," whispered Bickie. "Mmmm."

Emmy tried the wild spinach and to her surprise liked it. She also liked what she thought was chicken. "You try makande," she heard Bickie say to her as Emmy put her fork in the next experimental taste of new foods. Again, to her surprise, she liked the mixture of corn and beans.

Emmy ate in silence listening to the others at the table talk mostly about business and the coming venture to capture a rhinoceros for a zoo in Germany. The conversation interested her but not like the presence of Ellie sitting across from her along with the other woman who worked for Mister Mar's group, Annemarie. Emmy's first meeting with Annemarie still wasn't clear to her. Emmy had been brought back to the compound by Bickie after having been found on the river bank. It was Annemarie, the compound's combination veterinarian, nurse and medic who had checked Emmy out and treated both her skinned elbows and knees. She had also met the professional photographer, Ellie who was working on an assignment for something called C.R.O.W. which stood for the Concern and Respect of Wildlife. It was a branch of the World Animal Welfare League.

Ellie had been polite to Emmy when they first met, even assisting Annemarie in treating Emmy's scrapes. "Welcome," she had said, her eyes asking.

"My name's Emmy."

"Welcome to our little home in the Serengeti," said Ellie as she watched Annemarie cleanse the small girl's cuts and scrapes

Emmy heard the welcome enter one ear and, just as fast, it went out her other. She found she was held spellbound by the woman's presence, an exact duplicate of every picture Emmy had seen in the scrapbooks many times. Then, before Emmy realized, Ellie gave her a pat on the back and turned to leave.

"Nice meeting you, Emmy," she said. "I've got to make myself scarce so I can finish developing some film I took on our last capture." Just as she was about to exit through the doorway, she stopped and said, "I'll see you at dinner tonight, Emmy. If you'd like, maybe I could sit near you and we can talk."

Before Emmy could say a word, Ellie was out the door, her last words were, "My portable darkroom waits."

Emmy would later learn that the darkroom would be her bedroom.

Dinner ended with dessert that consisted of what looked like brown bananas covered in a caramel sauce. The fruit had been sautéed in butter and sprinkled with cinnamon. Emmy, with more of Bickie's gentle urging, tried the dessert. She ate it so fast that she drew the attention of the others especially Mister Mar who said, "Obviously, Missy, you didn't like Bickie's specialty of *imarikos*."

Emmy gave Mister Mar a blank look.

They all laughed even Ellie who smiled at Emmy and added, "You ate plantains," said Ellie smiling. "Good, aren't they? They're Bickie's creation and she serves them for only special occasions." She continued to smile and gave Emmy a pat on her shoulder. "You must be the special occasion. We all thank you for joining us."

"You're welcome, Gran..." Emmy blushed and lowered her

head. "You're welcome, Mam," she said politely.

Annemarie, who was sitting next to Emmy, leaned real close to her and whispered in her ear. "You ate bananas."

Emmy blushed.

"Come any old time," said one of the men at the table who was known as Buster

"You bet," added another man who Emmy heard called, Tab."

Emmy knew she had seen the two men before but couldn't place them. I know them from somewhere she thought as she smiled back at both men.

Mister Mar cleared his throat and silence set in at the table. "I'm sure you're all aware that we have several big, important contracts to start fulfilling as of tomorrow," he said. He began to smile. "I just got another one about an hour before dinner," he continued. "Some new guy contacted me. He's from back in the United States and is with one of those Chicago zoos. Any of you ever hear of a Walt Waveland?"

Emmy sat stunned saying nothing. That's my father's name, she thought. But, he doesn't work for any zoo. She paused and thought. At least I don't think he does.

"He wants bears, lions and tigers," continued Mister Mar. I think he also inquired about some cubs, rams and bulls." He stopped and looked at everyone at the table. "He wasn't specific as to what kind of bulls and I was too polite to tell him he should look in Spain." He gave me the impression that he might be building an ark." Laughter spread out from around the table. "But, before we can deliver that strange combination, we have to get a zebra for a customer in Portugal and also a rhino for that zoo in Germany." Mister Mar pushed his chair away from the table and stood up. "Early to bed folks," he said nonchalantly. "We've got a big day tomorrow." He looked down to the other end of table at Bickie. "Breakfast earlier than usual, Bickie," he said. "And fill your burlap sack for the afternoon," he said referring to, as what Emmy would learn, were sandwiches for lunch.

As Mister Mar turned to leave, Emmy's chair scooted back and she jumped up. "May I please go tomorrow, Mister Mar?"

"Too dangerous, Missy," replied the tall, strapping man giving her a way too serious look.

"Please, Mister Mar," said Emmy, not a single trace of pleading in her request. "I could take pictures. I could help Miss Ellie. I wouldn't be a pest," she continued, rattling off her reasons why she should be allowed to go on the hunt.

"Let her go," said Jean Claude. "She can ride with me and Ellie," he continued. "I'll look out after her." He let out a laugh. "I'd never have her ride with Bomba or Howdy," he continued. "And, in no way ever with Tab and Buster; those two guys think they're flying crop dusters instead of trying to corral a wild animal."

"Are you sure you want to go, Missy?"

Emmy couldn't sleep. She didn't want to close her eyes for fear of missing something; the sights, the sounds, the smells of the jungle, the Serengeti plains and even inhaling the air of Africa. She knew she heard noises outside but she didn't dare leave the safety of her bed. Bickie's words about only bad outside at night in the Serengeti stuck with her. Then, in the pitch black of her new room, somewhere in Africa in a vast place called the Serengeti, Emma Grace Waveland became homesick.

Gone were her feelings of excitement. Also disappearing were the urges to take millions of pictures. All Emmy now wanted more than anything was to be back with her parents. She didn't want to talk in Maasai; to ask questions in a foreign language. If she had a question she knew her parents would have an answer. They always did. She wouldn't have to be afraid of the dark. There was her lamp on her bedroom night-stand. That could be switched on whenever she wanted. She began to toss and turn trying to make sense out of what had happened to her. At one moment in her life, she was with her family on an African safari in Disney World. The next moment had her in the real Africa. How could that be she thought? Frustrated, she saw the answer to her question float just out of reach.

Her tossing and turning continued fueled by a parade of new faces that came crashing into her life. At first glance, those faces scared her. There had been too many too fast. There was the collection of men, all new but vaguely familiar. Way too familiar was Jean Claude. How could he be the safari driver in Disney World one day and be a driver capturing animals in Africa the next? She had taken immediately to Bickie, and wanted desperately to be friends with Luck and Far. The one person who fascinated her most was the lady photographer named Ellie. She knew the woman somehow was her great grandmother and she had several reasons as to why. Those reasons made complete sense to Emmy. First, the woman's name was Ellie. Second, she was a professional photographer. Third, and most important, she looked identical to every picture Emmy had ever seen of her Granna Ellie. What confused Emmy was that her great grandmother was dead, having died before Emmy was born.

Just as her eyes started to get heavy her nose twitched. Then it twitched again and again and again. She rolled over on her back, the lumpy, saggy mattress of the Murphy bed seeming to become her friend during the night and opened her eyes. All she saw was black. Then she realized that the door to her tiny bedroom that also served as Miss Ellie's dark room was indeed dark. She rolled out of bed and used the edge of her mattress to find her way to the door. There was a faint stream of light coming from under the door. She turned the knob and stepped into the hall to be greeted by luscious aromas. "Oh, my," she said aloud as her stomach began to let out demanding noises. She knew Bickie was in the kitchen even though the sun had just begun to peek over the vast grassy plain of the Serengeti.

Feeling a sense of bravado Emmy hurriedly dressed and without brushing her hair or her teeth—she had no brushes with her for either task—she walked down the darkened hall into the kitchen. She stopped in place when she saw Bickie, Far and Luck getting breakfast prepared with another helper.

"Well now, what do we have here?" asked a familiar pleasant female voice that made Emmy jump even though she immediately recognized the person behind the voice. It was Annemarie, the lady who had originally been referred to as, Miss Schnapps. Emmy had no idea what schnapps was.

"Say good morning to Miss Annemarie, Missy from River,"

remarked Bickie without taking her attention from the large skillet that was sizzling and popping, giving off a stomach growling aroma.

"Ah, yes," said Annemarie, her black eyes radiating a friendly smile. "My newest patient in the clinic yesterday and my delightful dinner companion last night." She took Emmy's hand and slightly turning it so she had a better view of her elbow. "And how are all of your nasty scrapes and bumps doing today?"

"I feel fine, Miss Annemarie," said Emmy, extending her other hand out. Even if she was hurting, she wasn't about to admit it for fear of not being allowed to go on the day's hunt for a zebra and a rhinoceros. She watched as Annemarie switched her attention to check on her knees.

Annemarie playfully mussed up Emmy's bed head. "Your wounds look like they're healing quite nicely," said the baby faced Annemarie, her pug nose twitched like a pet rabbit's while her narrow lips curled in a big smile, the ends almost reaching the corners of her playful blue eyes. "Emmy, what brings you to this part of Africa?" she asked.

Emmy's explanation flowed like the current of the river that had washed her ashore near Bickie's garden. She barely took a breath as she rambled on about Disney World, her mother, her father's driving, how mean her brothers were and how she loved taking pictures. When she had walked into the kitchen she had her camera bag slung over her shoulder.

"Well, it sounds like you've had a very unique wild adventure," said Annemarie. "Didn't she, Bickie?"

"Adventure, *aay-e*," replied Bickie. "Mister Mar, he say he try contact someone on de radio to help."

"I wouldn't need any help if I could get a signal on my iPhone," interrupted Emmy. She reached quickly into her camera bag and removed the phone. "See," she said holding up her iPhone for Annemarie and Bickie to see.

"That's a very pretty phone, Emmy," said Annemarie giving the phone a careful visual inspection. "It's got to be the most unusual phone I've even." She let out a brief chuckle as she turned the phone over several times in her hand examining it. "I bet you're very popular with the leopards," continued Annemarie as another chuckle followed, a big smile with it. "What I don't understand, Emmy, is where is the slot to insert your coin so you can make a phone call?"

Emmy didn't get the joke.

The four new women in Emmy's life were suddenly startled by a flash of light. "Oh, darn it," muttered Emmy. "I did it again."

Annemarie gave Emmy a questioning look and then her happy eyes looked surprised. "Is that me?" she asked pointing at the phone's screen. "Did that phone of yours take my picture?"

"I'm sorry," said Emmy. "It was an accident."

Bickie walked up alongside Emmy. "Show me."

Emmy did handing Bickie the phone. Another flash went off and Bickie was looking at her image in the camera.

Emmy laughed. "Oh, Bickie, you took a Selfie."

Before Emmy went into the compound's dining room for breakfast she decided to explore outside the kitchen. She had slid her iPhone into the side pocket of her hiking shorts after causing enough commotion to interrupt breakfast from being prepared. Annemarie and Bickie couldn't get over seeing their images on a screen that was also a part of a telephone. Far and Luck ended up sitting on the kitchen floor in a corner covering their faces with their hands after Emmy had snuck up on them, the camera's flash startling them as she took their picture.

This was the first opportunity Emmy had to see the compound since her hectic, unexpected arrival. She was like a sponge absorbing every detail of the frame building and the surrounding grounds. Emmy quickly discovered that there was so much to see and so much to photograph that she didn't know where to start. Her Rebel came out of her shoulder bag, the embroidered camera strap with pictures of Mickey, Minnie, Donald, Daisy and Pluto going around her neck and the telephoto lens being screwed into place with the turn of her hand. She went to zip up her bag and noticed that something wasn't right. She wasn't missing any cameras or equipment but somehow she had gained two more cameras. As she spread open wide the main zipper compartment there were her Baby Brownie and her Rollieflex, Ellie. She knew she hadn't packed them for the family vacation to Disney World, but they were there looking up at her appearing ready to be put to work.

Emmy heard Bickie shout out a word that sounded like

breakfast. Her camera went back into her bag. As she heeded the call, she decided to continue walking around the frame building to find the nearest door to the dining room. She continued to feel overwhelmed by so many new sights and sounds. The trees were different, few and far between, some alone, barely visible out on the grassy plain, while others, especially those along the trail she had first walked with Bickie, formed a jungle wall. There were animal noises that were new to her. The sounds of a host of colorful birds greeted her ears. As she came around the corner of the building she froze. So did a hyena. Emmy looked into the glassy dead eyes of the shaggy dog looking animal with the frightening teeth. Both human and animal stared at each other. Emmy didn't know why she did what she did next, but her hand slid slowly into the pocket of her hiking shorts. Out came her iPhone in slow motion. Her hand barely moved as she tipped the iPhone's lens toward the hyena who was still staring at her. Then the hyena didn't want to stare any longer and took a step toward Emmy. The only part of Emmy that moved was her finger that had been slowly brailing the face of her iPhone. Her finger tip found what she had been searching for and she gently pushed the button. A combination click and flash startled the hyena temporarily turning his eyes to a molten red. The hyena's interest in Emmy vanished and the animal turned and started to trot away deciding that, perhaps, Emma Grace Waveland wouldn't be on the day's breakfast menu. The ugly beast stopped once more, gave Emmy a curious look that kept her motionless, then turned and trotted away. Emmy let out a breath with a sigh after the hyena disappeared. Then she continued to look in earnest for the entrance to the dining room; this time doing it at a trot.

Several accelerated steps later found her bounding up the wooden stairs to the building's entrance. Once inside she took a look at her iPhone and the picture she had taken. "Wow," she muttered.

"What dis wow?" asked Bickie holding a tray filled with bowls. "You get in dare and eat before dat pack of hyenas in dare gulp down everything in sight. "

Emmy laughed and held up the camera for Bickie to see. "No time look what Bickie see all time," she said, sounding as if she were reprimanding Emmy. 'Now, dining room. Time for *anyaita edaa.*"

Emmy felt at home as she entered the dining room. She quickly found her same place she had the night before at the long table and sat down. She tried to hold a smile as she glanced around the table. The same faces from dinner were in their places. Seeing Mister Howdy and Mister Bomba again sent her mind whirling. She knew she had seen them before. She smiled at Jean Claude and wanted to thank him for helping to convince Mister Mar to allow her to go on the rhinoceros hunt. She quickly decided to wait until there weren't so many people around before she approached him. She smiled at both Mister Tab and Mister Buster and got the identical feeling that she had known them from someplace else or had at least seen pictures of them.

Mister Mar sat at the head of the table. At the other end of the table was Bickie. Seated next to Emmy was Annemarie with Ellie seated across from them. Emmy had all she could do to keep from fawning all over the photographer and not call her Granna Ellie.

Ellie surprised Emmy by greeting her with a big smile.

"Good morning, Emmy" she said cheerfully. "Did you sleep okay in that dark room of mine?"

"Oh, yes, Gran...." Emmy lowered her eyes. "Oh, yes, Mam," she said catching herself. "I slept real fine." She caught her breath and composure and turned into her usual bubbly self. "I took a picture of a hyena. Then Miss Annemarie had her picture taken by accident. Far and Luck even got their picture taken." She was gushing now. "And, you know what, Mam? Bickie even took a Selfie." Emmy's eyes almost bulged out of her head.

"A Selfie," repeated Ellie. "I'm not familiar with that term."

Emmy explained what had happened in the kitchen and excitedly reached into the pocket of her hiking shorts and pulled out her iPhone. Before she could continue her explanation of its workings, Mister Mar's voice interrupted her.

"There's a time and a place for everything, Missy," he said setting his fork down on the side of his empty plate. "Now is the time to eat." He paused. "And make all gone, Missy because you're going to need all the strength you can get when you come face-to-face with your first rhino." His stern look turned into a smile. "But, first, we're going to have to pick up a zebra for another client."

Emmy felt embarrassed but could feel her stomach jump with excitement. "Yes, Mister Mar. I'm sorry," she said her fork digging into the golden brown pancake looking food that was indeed a pancake; one made of ground roots from Bickie's garden. This, she thought, was so much more exciting than being with her family and watching her brothers pig out on energy bars and gulping down orange juice.

After breakfast Emmy saw Bickie give her a nod. She

politely excused herself and began to collect the dirty plates along with Far and Luck. In and out of the kitchen she went like a flash not seeing the smile on Bickie's face and a similar one on Mister Mar's.

The day was going so fast for Emmy that she didn't realize she was now walking with Ellie toward where Jean Claude was standing by a truck. Emmy had time to rinse out her mouth in the kitchen and rub her index finger over her teeth and gums in an effort to brush her teeth. Then her camera bag was over her shoulder and her Rebel's decorative strap around her neck.

"That's quite an interesting camera you have," said Ellie as she walked with Emmy toward the truck. "May I take a closer look?"

Emmy didn't know what to say. She just continued to walk while staring at the woman she thought she knew as Granna Ellie. Her mouth didn't move.

"I won't hurt it," Ellie said.

Emmy blinked. "Oh, I'm sorry," she stammered as she removed the shoulder strap with the Disney characters from around her neck and handed it to Ellie. "It's a Rebel," she said trying not to brag. "My father says it was named after me because I sometimes, according to him, can act like a stubborn brat. My mother dislikes brat so daddy changed it to, Rebel."

Ellie slowly turned the camera cradled in her hands examining every detail. She put the view finder up to her right eye and said, "Single lens reflex; very nice." The examination continued and then she looked at Emmy. "Thirty five millimeter?" she asked.

"Digital," Emmy shot back. "You get your picture right away," she continued to comment rapid fire. "You can get a series of pictures as fast as you can push the shutter and look at them right away. No darkroom chemicals to mess with anymore," continued Emmy. "I used to love to develop my own pictures. Print them too." She took a deep breath. "Now I just download my pictures to darkroom program on my computer at home and I can do whatever I want to them. It's so cool, Mam."

"Very nice indeed," said Ellie, more than impressed with her young companion knowledge of photography. "I'm going to have to get one of these," she said, a touch of envy in her voice. "When I get back to the assignment office I'll let my boss know that I've been out out here in the bush too long. The world's passing me by." She gave the camera another careful once over. "Very nice indeed, young lady," she said slipping her arm around Emmy's shoulder and giving her a gentle hug.

"Emmy, Mam."

"Emmy it is," said Ellie removing her arm and giving her young companion a wink.

Emmy's heart beat faster and her hands exploded like a covey of frightened birds being flushed from their hiding place. She managed to reach into her black shoulder bag, eagerness exploding from her face. Then she went weak. All she felt was shock. Her hand touched what it shouldn't have. Slowly she removed her hand from the bag. It was holding her Ellie, the camera she hadn't packed. Without hesitation she began to slowly explain to Ellie tha camera clutched in her hand. "This is still my favorite camera and very special to me," she said. "My great grandmother had one just like it. She was a photographer. My father told me that. I saw her scrapbooks. She took all kinds of neat pictures; even had a letter from a President of the United

States." She stopped and looked sheepish. "I'm sorry," she said softly. "I sometimes talk too much. That's what my father says. And, my three brat brothers," she added. She held out the camera to Ellie.

The professional photographer seemed to become swallowed up by nostalgia. "I had one of these when I worked for a news agency in Washington when I was young woman just starting out," she said, seemingly back in another time and place. "Incredible details in close ups. I loved working with it." She smiled at Emmy. "Now, because of the high speed action and the tough conditions I have to shoot under, I use a Minolta SR One." She reached into her own shoulder bag and brought out the 35 mm camera. "Kind of looks just like your Rebel, doesn't it?"

Before Emmy could respond she saw a red plastic object smaller than her little finger pop out from where the camera's shoulder strap was attached to Miss Ellie's Minolta. The object landed on the ground in front of Emmy's boots and her jaw dropped. Her eyes popped open so wide she thought they'd fall out of her head.

"I'm sorry," said Ellie, "I didn't mean to startle you." She reached down and picked up the plastic object from the ground where it seemed to have been looking up at Emmy. "This is so strange," she said as she twisted the tiny red and blue piece of plastic between her thumb and forefinger. "When I was your age, Emmy I was given this by my father and it became my good luck charm. I've had it forever." A look of melancholy washed over Ellie. "Then I kind of lost track of it over the years. I thought I had lost it." Her look turned serious. "I didn't realize until now that I still had it in my bag." She held out the object. "I'd like you to have it, Emmy," she said.

All Emmy could do was stare in disbelief. She couldn't move a muscle.

Ellie reached out, took Emmy's hand and placed the object in it. "Now don't you go and lose this," she warned.

Emmy continued to stare.

"Is something wrong, Emmy?" asked Ellie.

"I have a good luck charm just like it," said Emmy wrestling her hand into the pocket of her hiking shorts. She expected to feel the heat of the sailor boy like always, but her pocket was empty. She slowly pulled her hand out of her pocket. "I guess I must've forgotten it in the hotel room when we left for Disney World."

"Well, Emmy, you can have mine as a spare until you get back to your hotel," said Ellie with a warm smile.

Emmy's fingers closed tightly around the plastic object. "As soon as I find mine I'll send yours back to you," said Emmy. "Then we can both have good luck charms."

"A person, especially a shutter bug like you, can never have too many good luck charms," said Ellie.

"My father gave me the one I lost," said Emmy, her bubbly enthusiasm gushing out again. "He said it belonged to my great grandmother. He gave it to me. Called it a piece of junk," she said. Then caution disappeared. "It's really not junk," she continued excitedly. "It's magical. There's a picture of Mickey Mouse on the back. Well, it's just three circles, but it definitely looks like Mickey Mouse even though my father says it's a factory reject prize from a box of Cracker Jack."

Ellie's eyes reflected more than an interest in Emmy's magical Cracker Jack prize. Then the two photographers heard

Mister Mar's voice.

"Will you two ladies break up the sewing circle and get into the truck. Jean Claude is waiting," Mister Mar said. "We ain't got all day. Howdy, Bomba, Tab and Buster have a zebra and a rhino to chase down." He paused and gave Emmy a very serious look. "Are you sure you and your cameras are coming along, Missy?" he asked.

Emmy swallowed hard and said, "Oh, yes, Mister Mar I'm ready. And, I won't be a pest. I promise."

"She's in good hands, Mar," said Ellie. "I think she's going to be our good luck charm today."

Emmy saw Ellie wink at her,

"We're going to need more than good luck today," said Mister Mar as he pointed toward Jean Claude and his truck. "You two better get going."

Ellie took Emmy's hand. "We're all but gone, Mar."

"Good," replied Mister Mar. He looked seriously at Emmy. "Missy, I sure hope you won't get into Ellie's way," he began. She has a special seat for taking pictures. Just be sure you buckle up tight. I don't want to see you getting tossed out of Jean Claude's hot rod truck." He laughed and turned to look at Jean Claude. "Don't you go showing off and play stock car driver for our new little friend, you hear."

Jean Claude gave a shrug. "Never," he said. He looked at Ellie and Emmy and smiled. "Come on you two shutter bugs. There's a rhino out there on the Serengeti that I hear is a real ham in front of a camera. I hope you two are ready to satisfy his ego." He grinned at them. "As for me, I like the smile of a zebra. Much nicer teeth," he said, showing his own perfect teeth.

They heard the sound of a truck behind them and they turned to see Annemarie driving a truck that had a red cross painted on the driver's side door. The back of the truck was partially uncovered, the forward part shaded by a canvas tarp. Standing in back was four of the tallest men Emmy had ever seen. They were dressed in red, their attire similar in style to what Luck and Far were wearing.

Ellie saw Emmy's surprised look and said to her, "Maasai. They're coming with us to help with the captured animals."

As Ellie and Emmy got to Jean Claude's truck Emmy became almost a permanent fixture attached to Ellie's side. They got into the back seat of a converted truck that had a canvas top over the cargo area. Jean Claude turned around and said, "Strap up." He pointed at a pair of harnesses that had been commandeered from the cockpit of an old DC3 cargo plane. "I don't want Mister Mar getting mad at me if you bounce out of this truck while I'm trying to do my job."

"She'll be fine," said Ellie as she helped her much younger companion slip into the heavy harness and buckle it shut. "Be prepared to feel your bones rattle once Jean Claude gets in the chase."

If there was a bone in Emmy's tiny body, it did more than rattle. Emmy didn't care. She took so many pictures as the small convoy of vehicles rolled along the dusty road she didn't have time to realize that the road wasn't paved and had about as many holes as the entire African Continent had wild animals. She was in the midst of showing Miss Ellie how her iPhone's camera worked when their truck came to a stop. She looked up and saw the other vehicles form up into what looked like an inverted "V" formation. Mister Mar's pick-up truck was on the right hand side of "V" with Mister Howdy driving and Mister Buster was standing alongside the fender of the left hand vehicle with Mister Tab driving. Miss Annemarie would follow at the tip of the "V" driving her combination truck and mobile fist aid station with the four Maasai men in back.

Emmy had never seen anything like the two pick-up trucks before. Both trucks had the seat and back of what looked like the frame of a metal chair mounted to the fender; one seat on the right fender of one truck and the other truck had the seat on the opposite fender. Mister Mar and Mister Buster strapped themselves into their makeshift seats. Emmys lost her breath when she saw Mister Tab and Mister Howdy hand a long pole to each of the riders. The pole had a heavy rope loop attached. "Geez," she muttered loud enough for Ellie to hear. "It's almost like that *Hatari* movie dad got for us to watch in the van on our way to Disney World."

"Hatari," repeated Miss Ellie, giving Emmy a serious look. "Where did you learn that word?"

Before Emmy could reply Mister Mar's voice echoed across the grassy plain. "Saddle up," came his order. "Remember, we need a zebra first, a female and one that's healthy." There were nods and in moments, truck doors slammed and transmissions screamed out the shifting of gears as the trucks headed in the direction of what looked like to a giant cloud of dust off in the distance.

"Miss Ellie," she said politely. "Do you think it would be alright if I took some pictures? I won't get in your way. I promise. Do you think it would be okay?"

Miss Ellie put her hand on Emmy's shoulder. "Slow down, Emmy," she said. "Of course it'll be okay. Take as many pictures as you'd like." Ellie smiled at her and then turned serious. "Just you be sure and hang on to your fancy camera and everything else that belongs to you including your serious eyes and cute smile. They're going to be in for some real jolts."

"I don't jolt," shouted Jean Claude from behind the wheel as he shifted gears. "A bounce or two yes, but never a jolt."

Emmy couldn't believe how fast the truck was going and how the seat harness she wore dug into different parts of her body seemingly all at the same time. The truck did more than bounce. Jean Claude had lied. It did more than jolt. Sometimes all four wheels left the ground as he raced to keep up with the two trucks in front of him. Emmy clutched her Rebel and caught a glimpse of Ellie holding on to her Minolta, her eyes fixed on the dust cloud that now resembled a beige foggy cloak unable to cover the herd of animals galloping as if in panic. They were zebras. Instinctively, Emmy raised her camera to her eye. At that precise moment, the two lead trucks in the "V", poles and rope lassos sticking out like Knights of the Round Table jousting spears, made precise moves that scared one of the zebras from the herd. That's when Jean Claude turned the wheel of their truck so sharp that Emmy thought she was going to be tossed through the open air side. "Show time, Ellie!" yelled Jean Claude over his shoulder, and the truck broke from formation and raced alongside the other trucks as Ellie snapped picture after picture. Emmy, as if following Jean Claude's cue began snapping pictures, her automatic shutter whirling. She had to shoot across the interior of the truck at first, but she didn't care. Even the front windshield and Jean Claude's bush hat didn't bother her. She used them as foreground and backgrounds for the composition of her shots. The truck raced on bouncing and jolting her and she loved it. Suddenly Jean Claude was ahead of the trucks and she saw Ellie turn to shoot through the open back window of the truck. In an instant she twisted her body around and saw images in her view finder that she never knew existed. There was Mister Mar with his giant lasso reaching out for a galloping zebra.

Click, click, click went Emmy's camera.

Mister Buster came into her view finder. Click, click, click. Then both Mister Mar and Mister Buster joined the panting zebra and her camera continued to click. So did Miss Ellie's. Emmy hoped that at least a few of her pictures wouldn't be blurred from Jean Claude's driving. Her camera continued to click away as both lassos tightened around the zebra's neck and Mister Mar and Mister Buster released their seat belt harnesses. Jean Claude slammed on the brakes, shifted to neutral and jerked on the emergency brake. He was out the door in a flash jogging carefully toward the zebra that was jumping in a fit of panic. Jean Claude learned to be cautious after his very first day of driving when a wild animal's hoof caught him on the shoulder and opened up a gash. That was also the time when he held Annemarie's skill as a nurse and a vet in highest regard. She had kept him from bleeding to death.

Ellie jumped out of her side of the truck and continued to take pictures as she walked around Mister Mar and Mister Buster. Emmy, eager and anxious, struggled out of her harness.

Her door grudgingly opened with a series of groaning squeaks and she almost kicked her way out. She took a direction putting her opposite of Miss Ellie. Her camera was pressed to her face as she first knelt, then squatted and finally scooted on her butt and crawled on her belly to get different views and angles of the captured zebra.

Jean Claude had held onto the two lasso loops giving Mister Mar and Mister Buster a chance to subdue the zebra who was still fighting for his freedom. Emmy zeroed her camera in on the animal's face, the contorted mouth and panting tongue; the eyes screamed out a look of fear and panic, the straining of tendons and muscles. She couldn't click her lens fast enough. Then she saw Mister Tab and Mister Bomba jump from their trucks and run behind the truck Annemarie had been driving. Emmy saw an entire new series of exiting picture as the tailgate went down with a bang. The Maasai men leaped from the truck like giant graceful swans. Click, click, click went her camera as it captured Mister Bomba using a one handed vault to get into the back bed of the truck. Emmy instinctively knew that the scene unfolding was a photographer's gold mine; Mister Bomba would be the center of attention along with a dazed, but still very dangerous zebra. Emmy scampered behind and off to the side of the truck. She heard scrapes and scratches of metal as a large wooden crate appeared. The crate looked more like a cage with wide spaces between the vertical slats. Mister Bomba pushed the crate to the edge of the truck and gave a nod to Mister Tab who pulled a handle that started a tailgate platform up. Emmy's camera clicked. Then the platform stopped and Mister Bomba, with a huff and a puff, pushed the wooden crate onto the platform. As this was going on, Mister Mar and Mister

Howdy with Jean Claude's help and Annemarie's words of caution guided the reluctant panting zebra to the open end of the cage waiting on the platform.

"Nice and easy," Emmy heard Mister Mar say to the others. "Let us be nice and gentle with our new lady friend. She's looking like she might go into shock."

The zebra, near exhaustion, gave a final attempt at resisting, but was no match for the Maasai who gently guided her into the cage. Six sets of hands that included Annemarie's had positioned the wooden cage in the back of the truck while Maasai hands had it lashed securely in place. The entire process had been accompanied by a series of shutter clicks from the cameras of Miss Ellie and Emma Grace Waveland.

"Good work," said Mister Mar to the others. "Now let's get our lady friend home safe and sound," he said, nodding toward the zebra. "We don't want to lose her." He paused and looked out over the grassy plain. "We'll go after the rhino tomorrow. He walked over to Annemarie's truck where the zebra sat in the cage and talked to the four Maasai men who he had hired for the day to assist in the rhino capture. He said something to the men and they nodded as he held up two fingers. He gave a wave and walked back to where Jean Claude was standing by his truck. "I told the Maasai I would need them tomorrow. I said to their main man that I would pay them double." His head went from side to side then he looked at Jean Claude. "And no drag racing with some cheetah on the way back to the compound," he said then let out a laugh. "Besides, you always lose."

Jean Claude's laughter was louder than the others. "If you'll let me work on my truck's engine in my spare time, I'll whip any four legged animal in a race."

"Just keep that truck running," said Mister Mar. He turned and walked up to where Emmy and Ellie were standing. He looked at Ellie. "Did you get some good shots?" he asked. "I don't want those Crow people mad at us.

Ellie nodded. "If I didn't, then my little friend here got it all." She put her arm around Emmy's shoulder and looked into her eyes. "I bet your finger will be all black and blue tomorrow from all of your shutter clicking you did today." She smiled lovingly at Emmy. "I'm anxious to see your work."

Emmy beamed. "I can show you right now."

She never got a chance. "Saddle up!" she heard Mister Mar order. She felt Ellie's hand on her shoulder giving her a nudge in the direction of the truck where Jean Claude had already climbed in. The others, including Annemarie who had finished checking on the zebra, got into their vehicles.

Emmy noticed almost immediately that the ride back to the compound was different. Jean Claude appeared to have found a smooth, paved road even though there was none visible. Annemarie's truck with the caged zebra and the Maasai followed closely behind, both trucks barely hit a bump. They were going at a slower speed now and Mister Mar's and the other truck were far ahead of them, dark specks surrounded by clouds of dust.

"They need to get back to the compound to get things

organized for when we have to let the zebra out of her cage,"
said Ellie, noticing Emmy's concern that the others were almost
out of sight. She pointed at Emmy's camera. "Didn't you say
you wanted to show me the pictures you took?"

Emmy's eyes lit up. She was so excited that she almost
dropped her camera on the floor. Her camera was almost in
Ellie's face. "You look right here and you push this button if
you want to go to the next frame or push this button if you want
to go back."

Ellie suppressed a grin at her young companion's enthuse-
iasm. The suppression was also caused by her curiosity.
What's this shoot and view a picture on your camera almost
instantly, she thought? Her finger rested on the button Emmy
had indicated. If those guys back at the home office are keeping
this new stuff from me, she continued to think, I'll give 'em each
a bop on the head with my old Rollieflex." Her finger pushed
down. Then it pushed down again, and then again. She
glanced into Emmy's excited eyes and then pushed the return
button until she was at the start.

Emmy couldn't take her eyes off of Ellie. She couldn't
believe the parade of subtle expressions that were being flashed
across the older woman's face as her finger tip gently pushed a
button as if it were a fragile piece of priceless art. There was a
sign of amazement and then one of wonder. Emmy thought she
even saw pride. Ellie's finger continued to advance the pictures
forward and then return a series or a sequence for another view;
this time more analytical. Emmy saw her head go slightly from
side to side. Then she saw her camera come to rest in Ellie's lap
and the older woman give her a look she would never forget.
"Emmy, I don't know where you came from or who taught you

how to shoot pictures or where this new fangled piece of equipment came from," she said then pausing. "But, young lady, this is some of the finest work I've ever seen," she continued, raising her eye brows. "You're good," she said softly. "Real good."

Emmy glowed and wanted to snuggle next to who she knew was her great grandmother and idol, Granna Ellie. Her seat harness held her in place and wouldn't let her budge. There were no words spoken as the camera was handed back to her. None were needed. The excitement of the day finally caught up to Emmy and her eyes closed. The next thing she knew she felt her hair being mussed and she opened her eyes to look at a smiling Ellie.

"Wake up, sleepy head," said Ellie, her eyes filled with more than a smile. "We're back."

Emmy jumped up and looked around. All of the trucks were parked and lined up outside a fenced in area, theirs included. She saw Jean Claude directing Annemarie's truck with the zebra toward the gate entrance. Mister Mar and the others from the crew were inside the gate waiting for Annemarie's truck. Once in position, the men would pull on a lever that would raise the truck's tailgate so the caged zebra could be unloaded. Emmy saw Ellie unhook her harness and she did the same. With her camera bag strap securely over her shoulder and her Rebel dangling from her neck she was out of the truck. She held her Rebel at the ready not wanting to miss a thing while staying glued to Miss Ellie's hip as they neared Annemarie's truck. Mister Mar, his men and the Maasai were gathered at the rear of the truck.

The tailgate had barely stopped and Emmy started taking

pictures.

Ellie shook her head in amazement and grinned. "You are really something else, young lady," she said. The others were too busy to hear her. Annemarie wasn't.

"Is she a problem?" asked Annemarie, concerned. "Is she having a reaction to being separated from her parents?"

Ellie smiled. "Look at her with that camera. Does that look like someone who's upset?"

Annemarie smiled at Ellie. "Guess I stand corrected," she said.

They watched Emmy. She was in constant movement again shifting to her knees, then squatting, sitting and lying on her stomach. All the time her camera clicked away. "What's she taking pictures of?" asked Annemarie. "The zebra's still in the crate."

"That young lady has an amazing eye," replied Ellie. "I just saw examples of her creativity on the way back to the compound. She's an artist. No telling what she's seeing now, but I can't wait to get a look."

"Doesn't she have to develop her pictures?" asked Annemarie. "Are you going to allow her into your sacred dark room?" she said grinning at Ellie.

"No need," replied Ellie. "Kid's camera does that for her."

"Really?" asked Annemarie indicating she had been caught off guard.

"Really," answered Ellie, without taking her eyes off of Emmy.

A curious Bickie and even more curious Luck and Far had come out of the kitchen to see what Mister Mar and the others had captured. Bickie hobbled up to where Ellie and Annemarie were talking. "Da little one a problem?" she asked.

Ellie and Annemarie shook their heads gently from side to side several times.

"Mmmm," muttered Bickie as Luck and Far flanked her on each side, their bright red clothing adding color to the drab of khaki the others wore. All of them watched Emmy as if she were the only one in the compound. "Me wonder how polite girl end up in Africa." Bickie paused as if in thought. "She seem different dan us."

"I don't know about different," said Ellie, a slight smile forming. "But that young lady is a better photographer than almost every professional I've ever encountered. And I've met some great ones."

Annemarie nodded in agreement. "I never saw anyone with a camera, you included, Ellie who turned into a contortionist to get a picture." She began to laugh. "It reminded me of the time when Bomba, Howdy, Tab and Buster had to gather up those baby Gibbons that got loose when Luck and Far forgot to lock the gate to their cage."

The group started to laugh, but Emmy wasn't laughing. Her eyes were bigger than the plates that had been set at the dining room table that morning. "Granna Ellie," she tried to scream, but the two words came out in a whisper. "Miss Ellie," she said ever so polite. "Look over there." She turned toward the entrance to the compound, raised her camera and twisted the telephoto lens. Then her finger began pushing down as fast as the Rebel would allow.

Ellie, Annemarie, Bickie and the others turned. "Oh, oh," said Ellie calmly. "Looks like the new friends of Luck and Far are here for a handout."

Three elephants, a mother and two babies came racing into the compound trumpeting their arrival. Luck and Far ran to the little ones as the large female elephant stood close by.

"Are those two baby elephants hers?" asked Emmy without taking her eye from the view finder.

"One's a stray," Emmy heard Mister Mar say as he walked toward the women and the three elephants. "Her mother was killed by poachers," he said sounding both angry and sad. "This female here kind of adopted her." He walked to where Luck and Far were playfully petting the two tiny elephants. "Luck and Far seem to have adopted them. They've spoiled them on Bickie's leftovers," said Mister Mar. "They think those two Maasai friends of yours are their special chefs. Just be careful and don't get in their way or you might get run over." He nodded at Annemarie. "Our nurse vet found out the hard way, didn't you Annemarie?"

Annemarie blushed and Emmy's camera caught several different views. "And, my caution warning goes to you too, Missy with the camera that's bigger than she is," he said, staring at Emmy. "Do you understand?"

Emmy snapped his warning into the memory card of her Rebel. "Yes, sir, Mister Mar," she said, letting her camera hang down until it rested just below her rig cage.

"Good," said Mister Mar. "Now say hello to our visitors from the Serengeti. And be especially nice to the mother of those two babies. Howdy and Bomba found out the hard way by teasing her. She chased them into the garage where Jean Claude parks his favorite truck. When she got through there was a new door to the garage and Jean Claude had to replace a fender and pound out a bunch of dents from the truck's body."

Mister Mar shook his head like he couldn't believe what the big female elephant had done.

Emmy just stood, her camera hanging down, her mouth joining the camera. "Wow," she muttered. "Josh, you and Todd and Scott are missing the greatest vacation ever."

Dinner that night was filled with loud conversation. The excitement and feelings of accomplishment that the zebra acquisition went perfectly dominated the early part of the meal. Good natured joking and teasing soon took over. Emmy soon found herself in the middle of the laughter and the center of attention first by Jean Claude. He said, "Did you ever try to drive with a midget bouncing around in your truck like a soccer ball and all the time snapping pictures and landing on poor Ellie with every other click of her camera?"

Laughter and grins followed. "She was like a curious chimp on speed," added Mister Tab. "Squatting, kneeling, crawling like Big Bo, Bickie's pet rock python and acting like one of those burrowing rats in the desert."

"Oh, why don't you characters pick on someone your own size," said Ellie coming to Emmy's aid.

"By all means," said Annemarie. "You guys can be brutal at times."

"Us?" asked Bomba pointing at himself. Gee, guys," he said, grinning at the others. "Miss Peppermint Schnapps, the party girl, is accusing us of being brutal." His grin turned into a laugh.

"There was nothing more brutal than seeing Annemarie walking into breakfast the next morning after her birthday party."

The room exploded with laughter.

Suddenly Emmy's memory lit up and she remembered where she had seen Mister Bomba before. He looked like an old movie actor she had seen on cable television. Emmy had been mesmerized by movies that had been made when her parents were younger than she was now. She loved any story that had action. Love stories, well, they were for old people; old to Emmy was someone who was a junior or senior in high school. It didn't matter to her whether the film was in color or black and white; black and white holding a fascination for her. She was even attracted to old television, especially those shows in the infancy of television that were in black and white. Again, adventures were her favorites. Shows for little kids bored her even though she watched them.

The memory of a Mister Bomba was now crystal clear. He appeared in adventure movies that were about a boy who lived in the jungle; a young version of Tarzan. Mister Bomba could have been a twin to his namesake, the Hollywood actor, Johnny Sheffield who played the character, Bomba the Jungle Boy in several Class B Hollywood movies. It looks just like him she thought. Then her gaze shifted to Mister Howdy. A vision of him jumped into her mind from what she remembered was an old television show for children much younger than her. The television show was from before she was born and the primary characters were puppets and the main adult on the show was named, Buffalo Bob. She always thought that was a stupid name for an adult, but the kids in the audience loved it. Howdy Doody was the name of the show. Emmy couldn't get over how

Mister Howdy's face was a copy of the Howdy Doody character.

There was more laughter and Annemarie and Ellie got up from the table and walked to where Emmy was sitting. "Ignore them," said Annemarie. "They are mere male mortals." She smiled at Emmy. "They are at the bottom of the food chain here on the Serengeti."

"Amen to that," echoed Ellie. "They are so far at the bottom not an animal in the Serengeti or the crocodiles in the river would want one of them."

Emmy didn't laugh. With her recognition of Mister Howdy and Mister Bomba, her mind was about to spin out of her head. Suddenly, she startled the table by saying, "I want you all to be my friends forever."

Mister Mar raised his coffee cup in a toast to Emmy and gave her a reassuring nod. "Anyone who can turn into a contortionist to get a picture is a friend I'd like to have."

"Just teasing you about being a midget soccer ball," replied Jean Claude holding up his coffee cup in a toast. The others followed all of them stating, "Here! Here!"

Then everyone to Emmy's dismay started talking at once. That was unlike dinner at her house where her father orchestrated the conversations stopping only long enough to chastise one of his sons for poor manners or to allow Emmy's mother to give her opinion on a topic. Her opinion generally took over the conversation until she got up to serve dessert. That wasn't the case in the compound's dining room. In the midst of what appeared to be an argument between Mister Tab and Mister Buster, Emmy noticed Bickie nod in the direction of Luck and Far who had finished eating. The dishes vanished from the table and so did the two Maasai girls and Bickie. Moments later Bickie returned to the dining room carrying two porcelain coffee pots. She set one at each end of the table and gave a knowing look to Mister Mar before hobbling back to the kitchen. Mister Mar cleared his throat and dinner turned to business.

"Tomorrow folks we get to earn our keep," said Mister Mar. Then, before going on, he gave everyone at the table a serious look. "The zebra part of our job is done and, thank heavens, she's none the worse for wear. If she hadn't shown signs of possibly going into shock after her capture, we could've gone after that rhino. Tomorrow is our day for that and I've hired the four Maasai back to help us." He paused, shook his head and smiled. "Those guys drive a hard bargain. They want double for what I was going to pay them today. Their spokesman said they enjoyed the ride and watching the little one crawl along the ground taking pictures."

There was faint laughter from around the table and Jean Claude said, "You're serious about this rhino business aren't you."

Mister Mar nodded.

"Do you really dislike us that much?" asked Mister Buster, a slight smile forming on his square face that looked as if it had its roots somewhere were fjords were in abundance. "I hope you're going to provided me with a longer pole and let me ride in the back of Annemarie's truck with the Maasai."

"And I want an anti-tank gun," said Mister Howdy, running his right hand through his wavy red hair.

"After we finish here tonight," stated Annemarie, "I'll set up my end of the table for those of you who would like to donate blood for tomorrow."

Emmy saw Mister Mar's head go from side to side once, but his eyes stayed kind. Her stomach, however, felt as if it were going to jump out of her body. "Blood," she said softly to Ellie who was still next to her.

Ellie's hand stroked Emmy's hair. "Don't be afraid," she said softly. "It's just the crew letting their captain know that they understand the importance of tomorrow's hunt and that they'll be acting like the professionals that they are." She paused and gave Emmy a look that was more than serious. "I hope that finger of yours will be even faster than it was today." She smiled. "And don't you dare get out of the truck for better angles, Miss Shutter Bug."

Emmy blinked and tried to swallow. "Miss Ellie," she said being more than polite. "How did you know that's the name my father calls me?"

Ellie gave her a smile. "I didn't," she said, then playfully mussing her hair. "You're a photographer," she continued. "A photography nut. You're a shutter bug if I ever saw a shutter bug."

Ellie and Emmy heard Mister Mar clear his throat. They resumed paying attention.

"Now that I have everyone's attention again," Mister Mar continued. "Let me remind you that the Maasai are very savvy to the behaviors of our very large, horned unpredictable friend." He paused and looked at each person at the table. "I can't afford anti-tank guns for all of you." His eyes did a circle of the table. "We don't want what happened several years ago when we lost Chips. Remember, Annemarie?

Annemarie nodded from the other end of the now somber table.

"Even our nurse couldn't stop him from bleeding to death," continued Mister Mar. "Why old Chips thought he had to play matador instead of being a chase driver is beyond me." He stopped in reflective thought. "Jean Claude, you're every bit the chase driver that Chips was. If you want to chase after some jungle cat instead of getting in the way of one of those nasty brutes, you won't hear a word out of me." His eyes did the table circuit again. "Safety is our modus operandi for tomorrow and Missy," he stared at Emmy, "me thinkest you should stay here and help Bickie with whatever she needs helping with."

No one at the table believed what they saw happen next. Emmy shot straight up out of her chair. "Mister Mar, I will not stay behind. I'm just as...."

Miss Ellie finished Emmy's statement. "Let her sit with me like she did today. No harm will come to her. I promise," vowed Ellie. She smiled at the others sitting at the table. "Besides, she's one darn good photographer." Her open right hand reached out.

Emmy didn't hesitate. Her Rebel was in Ellie's hand.

"As soon as Mister Mar is finished with his briefing, I want all of you to gather around me and I'll show you what I mean about little Miss Shutter Bug here."

Emmy sat and watched her camera being passed around from hand to hand. No one said a word. What was spoken came from their eyes and the bulk of those expressions centered on awe, disbelief and admiration. Emmy's camera exchanged hands at least three dozen times until Mister Howdy blurted out: "How did you know that I stick my tongue in between the gap in my front teeth when I get tense?"

Emmy didn't have an answer.

"That's why you don't have any girl friends," stated Mister Bomba as he passed the camera to Jean Claude. "You look like a Halloween jack-o-lantern in need of an orthodontist every time you get serious around a girl."

Laughter filled the room and then awe, disbelief and admiration returned. The entire time Emmy could feel the warmth of her new Cracker Jack good luck charm. It appeared that Mickey Mouse's picture was flashing a warm smile from the pocket of her hiking shorts.

Mister Mar passed the camera to Annemarie who had moved from the other end of the table to sit behind him. Everyone in the compound knew that Mister Mar had an eye for Annemarie and vice-versa even though he was fifteen years her senior. Their relationship appeared to be a professional one of employer to employee which it was while they worked. They were more than friends at the weekly social functions that were held at the compound after five hard days of work. Mister Mar, however, still acted like the boss and only when he and Annemarie were alone did he show signs of affection. Emmy was oblivious to it all. What she knew was that she was going on a hunt the next day where a rhinoceros was involved, and she would be taking pictures alongside of her Granna Ellie.

Chapter 7

Emmy, her nervous energy gone from the excitement of the zebra hunt, slept as if she were in a trance. She found herself surrounded by wild animals of every conceivable type. The animals, however, did not act wild. They were tame, some docile and all friendly to her. Each one playfully nudged the other trying to get next to their new companion in the Serengeti. Emmy wanted to pet and cuddle with each one regardless of how big or small. And, she did. She was having the time of her life when the sunrise came through her open door blinding her. Puzzled, she thought, I didn't leave my door open last night. Something was wrong and she sensed it right away. She wasn't alone in her tiny cot. Whatever was with her was a bed hog; a large bed hog that was moving from the bottom of the cot to where Emmy's head lay nestled in her pillow. Emmy slowly opened her eyes and then wished she hadn't. She also wished that she hadn't gone to Disney World or had ever taken a picture in her life. She wanted to be back home, in her bedroom, throwing her Baby Brownie into the waste basket beside her night stand. Emmy wanted to scream. She wanted to run. She didn't know what she wanted to do so she did nothing; nothing, but look. And, what she saw told her that her life was about to come to an end.

Staring into Emmy's frightened eyes was a snake. But was it

a snake? Snakes, Emmy knew, slithered out of her father's vegetable garden. That was maybe once a summer and they were tiny, no bigger than a foot long, if that. They were green with a yellow looking stripe. This snake, her surprise bed hog companion, was bigger than a hog. It was bigger than Emmy. Emmy tried staying calm. That worked until the snake's tongue darted out. Then she let out a scream that scared the snake, her and everyone in the compound except Bickie.

The door to Emmy's tiny room had been ajar, but now it was wide open. Bickie stood in the opening. "There you be bad boy," she said, scolding the rock python, a non-poisonous African snake that wrapped itself around its prey, crushing it before consuming it whole. "Bo," she said, continuing to scold the monsterous snake who seemed to listen and cowar at the same time. "How many times I say you bed outside. No come in Bickie's home."

Emmy watched the snake slide from her cot and make its way across the floor stopping at the door and looking up at Bickie. "You bad, Bo," Emmy heard Bickie say to the snake. She lifted her hand, stepped out of the way and pointed at the open door. "*Shoma*," she ordered her eyes ablaze.

The snake obeyed and Emmy started breathing again. "Was that a real...."

Bickie nodded, the blaze gone from her eyes that had returned to being kind. "He name Big Bo," she continued. "He friend. Know I treat well. Feed live chicken. Other animals."

"Live chicken," repeated Emmy, slowly moving her feet under the blankets to be sure that there were no more surprises greeting her that morning.

"What's all the commotion?" asked Mister Mar as he joined

Bickie in the doorway to Emmy's room.

"Just Bo being bad," answered Bickie adjusting her white apron around her ample middle. "He scare Missy. She be okay."

Mister Mar gave Bickie a smile. "You and that Bo," he said sounding perplexed. "Don't I have enough problems with going out after a rhino today?"

"You be fine," said Bickie. She turned her attention to Emmy. "Get dressed," she ordered sounding like Emmy's father in a stern mood. "You eat plenty bickies today. You gonna need."

The only sounds in the dining room during breakfast were the assorted masticating and the smacking of lips over Bickie's biscuits and gravy and the occasional plea for salt or pepper or, in the case of Bomba and Howdy, the hot sauce; another Bickie specialty that most of the crew avoided because one drop could burn a hole in a cloth napkin. The quiet dining room made Emmy realize why Mister Mar had suggested the night before that she remain at the compound today to help Bickie. Today would be more than a safari, more than an adventure and more than an opportunity to take pictures. These pictures would be more than digital images on a tiny screen. They would be images of danger; the expression, life or death coming to mind. As much as she wanted to impress Mister Mar, her Granna Ellie and the rest of the crew with her photographs, she knew that obeying her elders and not being a pest were paramount.

Emmy's priorities, however, sometimes got realigned, especially if her cameras were involved.

The impact of the modern technology aspect of her photography equipment hadn't registered yet with almost everyone at the compound. It had with Ellie, but she was too busy in her darkroom after dinner broke up to dwell into the workings of Emmy's Rebel. Pictures had to be developed while Emmy was in the kitchen helping Bickie, Luck and Far. Getting her hands on modern equipment like Emmy's was definitely a must on her list.

As the crew silently sipped their coffee, Luck and Far got up and quietly began to clear the table. They didn't need a nudge from Bickie. They also knew that today would be different than most other days at the compound. A rhinoceros was not only respected by the Maasai like all of the wildlife on the Serengeti and the Ngarongoro Crater, but it was treated with an additional dignity reserved for an enemy warrior.

Mister Mar cleared his throat like he always did when he was about to speak, but this time he stood up and slid his chair carefully into place at the table. All the others did the same thing. Not one word was said even though Emmy had a lot of questions ready to pour out of her. She knew that there would be a more appropriate time and couldn't wait to get into the back seat of Jean Claude's truck and sit next to her Granna Ellie.

Then Mister Mar spoke. "Good luck and God speed," he said solemnly. Then he turned and started to walk slowly to his office. He stopped suddenly, turned and looked at the others almost glaring. "Be careful," he said like a father giving the car keys to his child who had just gotten a driver's license.

Emmy felt this would be a day she would never forget.

Even her new good luck charm in her pocket was generating more heat than her original one. Something exciting was about to happen in her life. She had no idea how exciting her life would become. No one did.

Ellie got in the truck first and got situated with her camera as Emmy slid in the seat next to her. Ellie smiled and gave her a pat on the head as she nodded at the heavy harness that had to be buckled up. There was an instant click. Then Ellie did something she didn't do the day before in the truck. She stuck both of her hands behind the heavy web binding of Emmy' seat belt harness and gave it a yank. Then she yanked at it again. Satisfied, her hands slipped out and she returned to readying her camera and equipment without saying a word.

Emmy heard the vehicles come to life. There was the shifting of gears and the convoy of hunters headed out following the same dirt road that they had the day before. They had traveled just long enough, the warm Serengeti breeze blowing through the open truck, to have Emmy's excitement turn to a sleepy tranquility. Her eye lids turned heavy and down went her head. The downward movement had Emmy's chin on her chest and a drowsy feeling took her over. Her eyes would pop open with each bump of the truck but she was never totally awake. Her eyes opened to stay when she felt Jean Claude stop the truck, the brakes eking out a long screech stating that they had done their job.

The other trucks had also stopped. The only sounds Emmy heard were the truck's engine being absorbed and carried in the direction they had come from by the breeze. She watched as Jean Claude got out of the truck and she reached for the safety latch on her seat belt. Ellie's hand kept if from going any further. Emmy looked but didn't say a word. Mister Mar and the crew were standing alongside of Annemarie's truck. They were talking with the quartet of Maasai men who were riding in the back. They were all stern faced. Mister Mar pointed in a direction at a right angle to where they had been driving. Two of the Maasai pointed in the same direction and said something that Emmy couldn't understand. Mister Mar shook his head, nodded where the Maasai had pointed and the conversation quickly ended. Truck doors slammed shut and the convoy started up again traveling in a new direction.

Emmy didn't have to glance at the truck's speedometer over Jean Claude's shoulder to see that the truck's speed had increased. Her harness was digging into her shoulders with each bounce of the truck, and each bounce seemed to gouge into her shoulders a little deeper sometimes making her feel as if she were being strangled. The jolting stabs didn't' let up and Emmy quickly discovered why. A glance out of the truck's open window on her sided told her that the truck had left any resemblance of a road. Emmy couldn't even see ruts. Waving knee high grass was their road. Emmy glanced at Ellie and she seemed disconcerted as she loaded a canister of thirty five millimeter film into her camera; the bouncing not seeming to bother her. She clicked the shutter a couple of times to advance the film and be sure there was a fresh frame ready for her first picture. Emmy remembered how she did that with her old Ellie camera when her father first showed her how to load it with film.

The truck continued to act as if were on a trampoline as it kept in line with the other trucks. The bouncing soon turned into a lullaby, a metronome clicking in time to the truck's springs and shock absorbers that had seen better days. Emmy soon found herself starting to dose off again. Her head went down, her eyes with it, but something was preventing her from sleeping. That something was her good luck charm that felt as if it were on fire. She reached down and rubbed her leg through her pocket and that's when she noticed that the trucks had formed up in their inverted "V" formation. She clutched her Rebel and hugged it to her chest.

"Relax, Shutter Bug," said Ellie with a smile. "No need to hurry. When that rhino decides to greet our party you'll have more pictures than you can handle." She gave Emmy a quick smile and then turned serious. "Now don't you forget about what I told you about not getting out of this truck," she said. "No matter what happens you stay put." There was a short pause accompanied by a way too stern look. "Understand?"

Emmy shook her head.

There was the sound of Jean Claude shifting gears and the truck started forward. "Hang on girls," he shouted over his shoulder. "We've got us a rhino in sight and he's a mighty big one."

Emmy strained to see but the dust kicked up by the other trucks blotted out most of what was ahead of them on the ground. She heard Jean Claude shift gears and the truck picked up speed. The truck was now bouncing like some out of control carnival ride. Emmy watched Jean Claude, the tightness of his jaw, the tension on his face, his eyes covered with a pair of aviator goggles. She reached for her camera. Not even Ellie who was next to her heard the series of shutter clicks.

The excitement grew along with the speed of the inverted "V" formation of the trucks. Emmy quickly understood the meaning behind what she had heard at dinner the night before when she heard Mister Howdy tell Mister Buster, "We ain't goin' after no stripped pony tomorrow, pardner."

Mr. Buster had nodded saying, "I saw what happened to Chips. You ain't gonna see me playing matador with the likes of no rhino."

Gears continued to grind away in a rapid series of shifts as the truck's speed changed dramatically at times going from almost a dead stop to speeds that had all four wheels leaving the ground as if the vehicles had turned into giant metal kangaroos. Emmy noticed Jean Claude maneuver the truck into position the way he did the day before. She could see the rhino churning along through the grass and couldn't believe how fast something so big could move. "He's gigantic," she said, awe coupling with her excitement. She looked at Ellie. "He runs faster than that zebra did," she said without taking her eyes off the lumbering rhinoceros. From her rear view of the rhino she could tell that he was over twice as wide as the zebra. "Gosh, I don't think he likes being chased," she said to Ellie who was continuing to photograph the hopeful capture and didn't appear to hear her. Then it dawned on Emmy. The last pictures she took were a sequence of Jean Claude. Her Rebel went to her right eye and she twisted, shifted and turned in her seat trying to get pictures of the chase. Then the rhino did something the others knew might happen, but Emmy almost dropped her Rebel. The rhino veered off course and went for the lead truck on the right trying to gore the driver's side door and also spear the driver, Mister Howdy with his giant, ugly horn. Mister Mar was sitting on the special exterior seat mounted on the right front fender. The tall, muscular man was strapped in, goggles covered his eyes and there was a white silk scarf across his mouth. His long pole with the lasso attached stayed in his hands as Mister Howdy spun the wheel to his left and met the charge of the rhino barely knocking him back on course.

"Wow," muttered Emmy her eyes appearing almost as big as the rhino was wide. Then she saw the rhino attack the truck that Mister Tab was driving. Mister Bomba was riding on the left fender exterior seat that looked like it had been taken from an old time farm tractor. It had. Mister Tab spun the steering wheel of his truck and it slammed into the rhino this time jarring him. The rhino's pace slowed for only a second before he turned his attention back to the truck with Mister Howdy driving. Mister Howdy was ready this time. Before the rhino could thrust his deadly horn into the metal of the truck, Mister Howdy shifted gears and spun the wheel hard to his left. His foot jammed down on the accelerator and the truck's custom made front bumper of welded pipe caught the rhino and lifted him off the ground. When the rhino came down his knees buckled. That, however, lasted for only a moment. The rhino shook off the collision and headed straight ahead picking up speed. All the trucks, including Annemarie's tailing the pack with the four Maasai on board, sped up and kept formation. Then, without a warning, the rhino stopped in his tracks and dropped to his front knees. He was panting and appeared to be gasping for breath. Mister Mar's hand went up and the trucks came to a halt still in their "V" formation, but now perilously close to the rhino. Mister Mar's hand was still up as he freed himself from his safety belt with his other hand. Cautiously, pole in hand, he came around the front of the truck. His steps were slow and precise. He gave a nod to Mister Bomba and he too slid out of his fender mounted seat. Pole and loop still in hand, his pace around the front of his truck was the same as Mister Mar's. Respect for the rhino coated with caution for their own well-being was evident to Emmy. Her camera was up snapping pictures. There was no rapid clicking of her shutter only long pauses as she framed each picture.

Annemarie had driven her truck just behind where the rhino stood. He was up and on all fours again snorting and pawing at the ground. Annemarie's brake lights came on when she saw Mister Mar's hand signal her. In moments the four Maasai were out of the back. Each had a similar loop and long pole. Like Misters Mar and Bomba, they cautiously approached the rhino from behind all keeping equidistant from the other. The rhino was almost surrounded with Mar and Bomba not quite in front, but staying off to the side in case the rhino started up again.

Emmy never saw the signal from Mister Mar, but she saw the almost instantaneous results. Six lassos were around the rhino's neck and pulled tight. The beast bucked and struggled. He snorted and tried to charge at Mister Mar, but five others held tight. His efforts were switched to Mister Bomba, but with the same effect.

Ellie was now out of the truck and snapping pictures. She stayed well behind the men who had the rhino totally surrounded. They watched as Mister Tab had gotten out of his truck and approached the rhino from behind. He was carrying a heavy rope. On the other side of him was Mister Buster. The heavy rope had what looked like a large knot at the end. Mister Tab coiled the rope in one hand and grabbed the knot in the other. He took several steps toward the rhino's rear legs, squatted down and tossed the rope, knot first under the legs of the massive animal. Mister Buster grabbed the knot as it bounced off the ground like the way one of Emmy's brothers might have fielded a ground ball playing back home in their summer league. He took the rope and quickly ran around the rhino toward Mister Tab who was on his way to meet him. The knot exchanged hands and quickly became another loop with the slack taken up until the rhino's rear legs were being squeezed together.

"Hey, Buster," called out Howdy to his partner who was holding onto one of the ropes around the rhino's pulsating neck, "who said this old boy don't know how to hog-tie some old jungle critter?" He pulled the loop of rope around the rear legs of the rhino tighter as if he were competing in a rodeo.

Emmy was stunned by what she saw and she made sure her camera captured every exciting moment. Then the tomboy and rebel in Emmy took over. All of the earlier warnings joined her promises of not to get out of the truck and were now scattered by the Serengeti winds. The truck door groaned its way open and she was out of the truck running toward the rhinoceros her camera clicking as fast as she could click it to capture the action developing before her eyes. Before anyone realized, she was almost next to the rhino. She knew what to do and so did her index finger. Click, click, click went the shutter.

The giant rhinoceros appeared to stop struggling. Several snorts escaped him as his head went slowly from side to side several times then stopped when he saw Emmy. His eyes never left Emmy. His large head pointed at Emmy as if he were taking aim; his nasty looking horn pointing at her as if she had a bull's eye painted on her t-shirt. She didn't notice and didn't seem to care. Her thoughts were on taking pictures. I'm taking pictures of a real live rhinoceros, she thought. Geez!

Click, click, click.

The rhino didn't care about Emmy's creative picture taking techniques. He didn't care if six nooses were around his neck and that his hind legs were being tied tightly together. As Emmy clicked her shutter and Ellie did the same as well, the rhino became camera shy. He also found a strength the others didn't anticipate. The strength was also accompanied by a nasty streak. The rhino seemed to explode, his body tossing and turning in six different directions at once. Ropes were ripped from the hands of the four Maasai. Gloves saved the hands of Mister Mar and Mister Bomba from severe rope burns. Mister Tab and Mister Buster didn't fare so well. The rhino's hind legs shot out. Before anyone could recover, the thick rope that was once coiled tight around his legs now lay useless on the ground. Six other lengths of heavy rope lay on the ground, the nooses still around the rhino's neck. There were several snorts and the rejuvenated animal headed for Mister Mar who wasted no time vaulting over the hood of the truck just as the rhino rammed into the front fender. Mister Mar's commands came out fast and furious. They weren't necessary. The rest of the crew sought shelter in the nearest trucks. Not Emmy. She kept taking pictures.

The screams to get inside the trucks continued and Emmy seemed oblivious to what was going on, her body seeming to turn into a dozen different positions all at once as her finger pushed at the shutter of her camera. Then she saw the eyes of the rhino glaring at her through the telephoto lens of her camera. Oh, oh, she thought as her face appeared from behind the slowly lowered camera that came to rest on her chest; the large lens pointing directly at the rhino's horn. Oh, oh, she thought again. I don't think he likes me.

The rhino continued to glare while a front hoof pawed at the dusty ground. A smile seemed to appear on the animal's face. Emmy wanted to run, but the rhino was too close. She would never get to the safety of any of the trucks no matter what route she took and how fast she ran. Then she heard Mister Mar.

"Don't move a muscle, Missy," he stated calmly as if he were addressing his crew in the dining room after a meal.

Emmy froze. She could see Mister Mar coming out from behind the protection of his truck. Mister Bomba had emerged from behind his truck. Both men carried poles with fresh nooses attached. She wanted desperately to take pictures of what was going on but knew those might be the last pictures she'd ever take. What she saw next made her knees shake. Annemarie had entered her field of vision. She was carrying a rifle. "Oh, no," thought Emmy. She saw something attached to the barrel of the rifle. It looked like a tiny harpoon with a small cylinder attached. She watched as Annemarie inched very slowly into position, her feet barely touching the ground. The other crew men approached the rhino from the front. Then, without warning, they all started to whistle and holler trying to take the rhino's attention away from Emmy. It didn't work. The rhino wanted Emmy. Then the four Maasai went into their tribal jumping ritual. Their bright red neck-to-ground wraps flapping as they seemed to all take vertical leaps of over four feet. Emmy thought they were going to jump over the rhino. It didn't take more than several jumps before the rhino turned and let out a snort. He was now facing Mister Mar. The group's boss stood erect, all six feet plus of him presenting a formidable foe to the rhino. The rhino wasn't impressed. Mister Mar stared directly into the eyes of the agitated beast. The rhino stared back. He appeared to be doing his own calculating. Before the rhino could take a step, Annemarie fired the rifle. The needle of the cylinder contained a tranquilizer. At first the rhino didn't care. He started to charge for Mister Mar. That was his mistake. Mister Howdy hurled another noose around his neck. The Maasai stopped their jumping and scrambled to gather up the loose ends of the ropes that were already around the rhino's neck. They all pulled hanging on with every ounce of strength they possessed.

Soon the tranquilizer took effect and the rhino's legs gave out. He seemed to drop to the ground in slow motion, a long combination of a snort and a grunt coming from him that was also in slow motion. All nastiness had vanished from him as he crashed to the ground with a ground quivering thud. His eyes glazed over as he lay on the ground in a daze.

Emmy still hadn't moved. Then she heard Ellie's voice repeating what Mister Mar had said to her earlier. Then she did something she always prided in not doing. She started to cry. Then she heard Ellie's soothing voice say to her: "You can't get a clear picture through that view finder of yours if your vision is all blurred from your crocodile tears. Then she heard the shutter on Ellie's camera click. The backs of Emmy's hands wiped across her cheeks and eyes, a series of a combination sniffles coupled with hic-cups followed. Then the twelve year old forgot about her age; forgot that she should be scared to death like all twelve year old girls; like any human being coming face-to-face with a rhinoceros. The backs of her hands wiped her eyes one more time and then those same hands went into action with her camera.

Click, click, click.

Annemarie had returned to her truck and backed it up to where the rhino still lay in a tranquil drug induced state. The Maasai had a large wooden crate off the loading bed of the truck and were positioning it so that they and the others could slide the massive animal into his new quarters for the ride back to the compound.

"He won't come out of the dosage I gave him until we have him cooped up in that special pen back at the compound," Emmy heard Annemarie say to the others; Mister Mar specifically.

"Be careful," said Mister Mar to the others as ropes were being pulled and a mixed crew of Maasai and the drivers pushed from behind. The entire crew began to chant in unison: "One, two, three! Load!" The chant was joined by sounds of muscles being pushed to their limits. Then the chant was repeated. None of the crew heard shutters clicking from two cameras. They didn't care.

Emmy fought the urge to get as close as possible to the rhino. She knew that she had exceeded being a pest and, if Mister Mar ever told her father what she had done, she would be in big trouble. Emmy glanced down at her telephoto lens and knew there was no reason for her to get any closer to the rhinoceros even though she had been told the beast was a vegetarian. I don't think he's looking at me as if I were a serving of Bickie's makande, she thought. She quickly twisted the barrel of the large lens that seemed to bring the rhino's nose up to her own. Bickie should have told me that night wasn't the only time when bad things happen on the Serengeti, she thought as she continued to twist and slide the lens for another picture. For several pictures she was on her knees; several more came from her being on her belly. In the next instant she was standing on Mister Mar's special seat mounted on the fender of his truck. She almost lost her balance but fought threw it and snapped the pictures she wanted.

It took the crew almost a half hour to get the caged rhino into the back of the truck. Emmy could see the special attention that Mister Mar, Annemarie and the others were giving to the position of the crate and its cargo in the truck. Several of the nooses had been converted into tie-down ropes securing the crate. Other nooses had been fitted around both the front and back legs of the rhino and then securely tied to steel rings on the sides of Annemarie's combination ambulance and animal hauling vehicle. "I don't think our mean friend here is going anywhere," Emmy heard Mister Mar say to the others. Emmy could see that his eyes were looking at Annemarie. The next words out of Mister Mar were, "Okay, saddle up."

The ride back to the compound gave Emmy an eerie feeling. First was the change in drivers with Annemarie and Jean Claude changing vehicles, Jean Claude now chauffeuring the rhinoceros. Annemarie was driving Emmy and Ellie. The second eerie feeling came from Ellie's silence. The only communication she had with Emmy was a finger pointing at her seat belt to be sure that it had been fastened. All the time during the slow ride back to the compound Emmy could feel her good luck charm in her pocket generating heat.

Jean Claude was driving with the utmost caution, his main concern was not to bounce around or jostle their precious cargo. He was leading the convoy of vehicles followed by Annemarie and flanked by the trucks with Mister Mar, Bomba, Howdy, Tab and Buster. Their trucks were so close to Jean Claude's that they could reach out and touch his doors.

At one point, the heat coming from Emmy's pocket made her cringe. She rubbed the good luck charm Miss Ellie had given her. "Ouch," she muttered, the heat coming through the pockets of her shorts sending her a message she knew had to be obeyed.

Ellie didn't seem to notice and continued to gaze out of the window not saying a word.

Soon the compound came into view as did the figures of Bickie, Luck and Far. Emmy's eerie feelings seemed to vanish. Gone was the heat in her pocket. She found herself checking her camera and dusting off her lens with a small soft bristle brush she had taken from her shoulder bag. As she finished, the truck with the rhino stopped and Jean Claude began to back the truck into a special corral surrounded by a high iron fence. The Maasai quickly jumped from the truck while the other vehicles lined up outside the gate. Emmy watched Mister Mar and the others get out of their vehicles and gather behind the truck with the rhino. One of the Maasai sent the tailgate up, stopping it when it was flush with the cargo bed of the truck. Several of the Maasai climbed up on the bed and disappeared into the back of the truck. Ends of heavy rope were tossed out the back and she saw Ellie open her door. She wanted to open hers but didn't dare, Ellie's look of admonishment still fresh in her mind. Her hands nervously traveled along the camera's frame, her fingers touching every inch of the surface. She was the only one outside of the corral. Even Bickie, Luck and Far were inside. She couldn't stand it.

The truck's door opened and Emmy's feet barely touched the ground and she found herself hiding behind Bickie, Far and Luck hoping that none of the others would see her. True to form, Emmy raised her camera making sure the three heads in front of her were not blocking her view. Her shutter clicked several times and those several clicks were enough to abandon her hiding place. The shutter bug went into action

None of the others seemed to notice Emmy. They were all concentrating on unloading their precious and very dangerous cargo. Emmy was savvy enough to keep her distance relying on the features of her telephoto lens to give her the pictures she wanted. Her finger pressed on the camera's shutter time and time again, rapid fire sequences being clicked off. There was the wooden crate positioned on the tailgate, the strain of neck and shoulder muscles visible from the Maasai. Signs of tension showed on Mister Mar's face as he barked out his directions. With each gesture, with each order, Emmy's finger punched in a pictorial record. Then she concentrated on the personalities of Bomba, Howdy, Buster and Tab. Each showed a different side of being serious while doing their jobs. Emmy found herself instinctively positioning herself to get a different and better angle for her pictures. She wanted a variety of backgrounds and got them any way she could. She was back to lying on the ground then climbing on the roof of the truck's cab like a human mountain goat. Her shutter kept clicking.

The wooden crate with the rhino was now on the ground and the crew moved with caution as skilled Maasai hands reached into the crate like cage and removed the ropes from around the rhino's front and back legs. The ropes were quickly coiled and placed outside the fenced in area's heavy gate. Mister Mar gestured to the others to vacate the corral.

Bickie, Luck and Far went first, Bickie's arms around each of the girls' shoulders. Annemarie, Bomba and Howdy followed. Mister Mar gave a nod and Tab and Buster joined him at the sliding door opening to the cage. No one said a word but they knew their jobs. Ellie backed away, her camera clicking. None of them noticed Emmy who was now lying on the top of the canvas truck, her head down, finger pressing on the shutter as fast as she could and balancing precariously close to falling off on the cage.

Just as Mister Mar reached to pull the pin on the gate to the cage, he gave a nod to Tab and Buster. Another nod saw Howdy and Bomba at the outside gate to the corral, Bomba grasping the gate and Howdy ready to latch it the moment Mister Mar cleared the pen. As Mister Mar lifted the heavy metal safety pin and removed it from the cage, he took his first sprint step toward the gate. That's when three things happened at once.

Ellie saw something in her viewfinder she couldn't believe. It was Emmy. She let out a shrill, "No!"

Emmy had learned forward to get a better angle of Mister Mar's thick fingers lifting the pin on the cage. When she heard Ellie's scream she lost her balance. What she remembered next was she had landed on top of the cage on her back. She was dazed and out of breath but protecting her camera, her arms cradling it, the lens pointing at a puffy white cloudy African sky.

As Mister Mar was taking his second spring step toward the gate, the rhino came out of his drug induced coma. He was not pleased.

Emmy rolled over, her toes pointing down at the cage's opening. She thought about scooting backwards, jumping off the cage and making her way to where the entire crew, except Mister Mar, was standing. They all looked stunned. Then Emmy felt the same way as she found herself being greeted by the rhino's large ugly horn inches from her pert nose. "Oh, no," she blurted out. Then she felt herself being grabbed by her ankles and being pulled off the cage. Before she realized, she was on Mister Mar's shoulder being carried like a sack of grain.

Mister Mar ran like the fleet footed halfback he once was for USC. Suddenly, the injury that took away his football stardom returned to give him a message. The message was that he should have had the operation the doctors suggested back in college. Now, his right side seemed to crumble. It was same side where Emmy lay draped over his shoulder. Mister Mar tried to use the strength of his left side to compensate for the weakened muscles on his other side. There was no compensating. Mister Mar and Emmy tumbled to the ground.

The rhino's unhappiness at being caged exploded. He began to imitate a Brahma bull kicking and gyrating out of a chute at a rodeo. The wooden cage came apart as the rhino kicked and thick wood turned to splinters. The rhino's kicking soon resulted in two new entrances being added to the cage. Entrances didn't interest the animal. He hated the cage and made every effort to show the amount of his hatred. Several whirling kicks later he had his wish. The cage was gone.

"Emmy!" yelled Miss Ellie.

"Granna Ellie," yelled back Ellie, a look of fear coated with panic accompanying her yell as she tried to get off of Mister Mar's shoulder.

"Damn," said Mister Mar as he used his good leg and both hands to drag himself upright. Emmy was still balanced on his shoulder, her arms around his neck and her idea of getting off his shoulder and making a mad dash to where the others were standing safe vanished. She wasn't about to let go. Mister Mar quickly evaluated the seriousness of what not only happened but what could happen. None of what he evaluated had a happy ending.

Tab and Buster sprinted into the corral with Howdy and Bomba close behind as the angry rhino was also giving his own evaluation of the situation. A big enemy with a little enemy on top now held his concentration. He pawed at the ground and his snorts sounded like a bugler blowing charge.

Tab's bush jacket came off and was in his hands and he looked like a matador about to fight El Toro in the Plaza de Toros.

Buster began jumping up and down, waving his arms and shouting out choruses of, "Yea, yea, yea!"

Howdy and Bomba circled the rhino putting themselves in the farthest distance from the gate and behind him.

The rhino had not taken his eyes off of Emmy and Mister Mar. He was now snorting with a fury. He had his prey and nothing was going to stop him this time. He didn't consider Bickie, Far, Luck and the Maasai. No one did.

Before any of the others, including the rhino, realized, the four Maasai men clad in their traditional red garments entered the pen and once again began their ceremonial jumps. Luck and Far began waving their arms like Buster while Tab moved in a position in front of the rhino, his jacket at the ready like a matador's cape.

Bickie, who had been accused by villagers of practicing bad medicine when she was younger, before she had lost part of her foot, limped toward the rhino, her eyes staring into the eyes of the beast. She held an object in each hand, the objects were the size of two flattened baseballs.

The rhino charged forward out of control then stopped and spun around. There was a new charge and then a wild turn in still another direction. Dust and dirt were kicked up in chunks. The crazed rhino didn't know who to attack first and it would only be a matter of seconds before he made up his mind. He was beyond furious and nothing or no one could stop him.

Mister Mar used his weakened leg to help with his balance as he put all his weight on his good side and started to hop toward the gate. Emmy was on his shoulder looking back at the rhino. "Oh, no," she screamed when she noticed the rhino had made up its mind who he wanted.

Instinctively Emmy pointed her camera at the rhino, engaged her flash and began shooting pictures as she bounced on Mister Mar's shoulder. Bright, blinding light lit up the compound's corral and momentarily blinded the rhino.

Annemarie and Ellie waited at the gate ready to slam it shut once Mister Mar and Emmy were safe. The others were agile enough, except Bickie to climb the fence and get to safety.

Bickie walked slowly toward the rhino her eyes never leaving the rhino's eyes as the Maasai men continued to jump, some of their jumps appearing to almost launch them over the fence. The red garments of Luck and Far continued to flap in the Serengeti wind as Bomba and Howdy got closer to the rear end of the rhino. They had picked up the ends of two ropes sticking out of the cage and were quickly fashioning a noose on each rope.

Suddenly the rhino stopped moving. Everything stopped moving except Bickie. She was now within an arm's reach of the rhino. A deathly calm fell over the compound. The winds stopped blowing. The only sound came from Bickie's one foot that dragged along the ground. Then another sound was heard. It was faint at first, but it came from Bickie. It was a chant. Bickie still held the objects in each hand and she moved them slightly from side to side as if she were teasing the beast. Then her chanting increased in intensity and the only movement inside the pen was Bickie.

When the Maasai men heard the chanting, they stopped jumping. As their bare feet hit the ground, they seemed to freeze where they landed. Far and Luck also stopped trying to distract the rhino when they heard Bickie's chants. They began to slowly back toward the open gate where Mister Mar had limped through with Emmy on his back her finger never stopping on the shutter button for a second. The Maasai men along with Far and Luck retreated to safety, clearing the gate but never taking their eyes off of Bickie and the rhino.

Mister Mar gently set down Emmy without a word. She appeared oblivious to the danger and kept taking pictures. Annemarie and Ellie came to her side, but she didn't seem to notice. Mister Mar got the attention of the Maasai men who quietly gathered around him without making a noise. He also saw that Tab and Buster had picked up two more ropes. All Mister Mar did was nod in the direction of where Bickie was now face to face with the rhino and the Maasai men, as well as his crew, knew exactly what to do.

Bickie's chanting had continued until it sounded as if she were yelling at the rhinoceros as if he were a naughty delinquent child. Her chant then reached a crescendo and stopped. The hot, dry Serengeti air still remained deadly silent. No one moved; no one except Bickie. She reached out and placed the objects she had been holding in her hands directly over the rhino's eyes. As if by magic, the rhino's legs gave out and he crumbled to his knees. Bickie began to chant again and the two objects slid off the rhino's eyes landing on the ground in front of his drooling mouth. In an instant four nooses had the rhino from the front and back. The only parts of the beast that moved were his tongue and his mouth as the two objects Bickie had dropped in front of him disappeared into his mouth.

Emmy's camera recorded it all.

Dinner that night was later than usual. Bickie stayed confined to the kitchen, her ever present chatter and laughter missing as if sucked out of the compound by a vacuum. Far and Luck also stayed in the kitchen. They killed time by swatting at several pesky flies with oval shaped paper fans fastened to short wooden handles. They were waiting for any type of order to start serving.

The entire crew including Emmy used the time to finish the job of securing the rhino as they waited for Mister Mar. He was in Annemarie's quarters where a small alcove off her bedroom served as the compound's infirmary. Annemarie had put the finishing touches on a walking cast giving support to Mister Mar's strained side. "Okay, Southern Cal Trojan with the bum leg," she said trying not to smile. "That should hold you for awhile. No work for a couple of days."

"Sure, Daktari," said Mister Mar a sarcastic smile accompanying his acknowledgement. "I'll take it easy after we get our horned friend out there delivered into town." He paused and looked sheepishly at Annemarie. "Thank you," he said meekly. "Maybe you can help me when we get to town about finding out about our little girlfriend's parents."

Annemarie pointed at the door. "Enough talk, Jungle Jim. I'm hungry."

After Bomba, Howdy, Tab, Buster, Jean Claude and the Maasai men secured the rhino in the pen they had all congregated outside of Annemarie's infirmary room to wait for their boss. They had driven the truck out of the pen and also removed all traces of the shattered wooden cage. The rhino, for some unknown reason, never moved from his spot. His tongue was the only part of him that stayed in motion and that was to continue to lick at the ground where Bickie had tossed the two objects. He had devoured the objects like an old ravenous pet dog.

After her mysterious encounter with the rhino, Bickie had turned and walked out of the caged area appearing as if she were in a trance. Her eyes were like two red hot coals and her chanting continued although barely audible. Only the Maasai, including Luck and Far, knew that Bickie's chants had to do with medicine, a special medicine most times used to treat the good and sometimes to thwart bad and evil. The Maasai who lived near the compound and were hired a number of times during the year by Mister Mar knew that Bickie was more than a cook. They knew she possessed powers that that no one else in the tribe or surrounding tribes and villages had. Bickie, it was rumored, had stopped three poachers from further annihilating rhinos and elephants for the ivory. The poachers made the grave mistake of trespassing on the Maasai lands and killing the wild animals that the Maasai revered and respected. No one knows exactly what happened to the poachers, but they were found dead. There were no marks on their bodies and the only witness, a young boy in hiding to conceal the pain of his having been circumcised as a rite of passage, swore that a woman, one who had half a foot, surprised the poachers. As his story went, they laughed at her and pointed their weapons at her. Their laughter stopped when she pointed both hands at them, her thumbs extended down, stared and began to chant. The young boy said he could see her eyes turn red and almost burst into flames. His story went on that the poachers dropped their weapons, each appearing that they had seen a devil. The woman continued to point and chant, her chant getting louder and louder. The boy knew that the woman had put a curse on the three men as he watched each of them grasping at their throats, their eyes getting so big they almost popped from the sockets. The boy finished by saying he saw agony written all over their faces. "They died still kneeling, looking as if they had turned to stone."

After walking from the fenced in area, Bickie returned to the kitchen with Far and Luck at her side. She worked in total silence communicating with the two girls by head nods and hand gestures. When she saw Mister Mar and Annemarie through the kitchen window approaching the dining room she looked at Luck and Far and said: "Serve food before it breakfast. Bickie no have all day."

Emmy had spent the entire time wrapped in Ellie's arms crying into her bush jacket and apologizing for not obeying. "I hurt Mister Mar," she sobbed. "It was my fault; me and this stupid camera. I wish I've never taken a picture in my whole life."

It took some time, but Ellie finally calmed Emmy down. She stroked her hair and said, "Your camera is not stupid." She continued to try and comfort Emmy saying, "You've taken some of the most beautiful photographs I have ever seen in my life. " She felt Emmy sniffle some more and then look up at her. She stroked her hair and said, "Why don't you show me all of those pictures you took before, during and after meeting that nasty rhinoceros and let me judge how stupid they are?"

Emmy choked back more tears and slid off Ellie's lap where she had been sitting letting out her grief. Her camera bag and her Rebel were on the floor nestled against her dusty sand stained hiking boots that she hand kicked off. She was hesitant as she picked up the camera and handed it to Ellie. "I know they're all stupid," she said softly then bursting into tears again.

"There is no such thing as stupid," said Ellie to her as she pointed back to her lap. "Now take your seat and let's take a look at what you saw through that view finder of yours today."

Emmy watched each picture seem to come to life on the camera's tiny screen. She waited for Ellie to say something to her, anything, but Ellie wasn't talking. She couldn't talk. All Emmy felt was the woman's body twitch as each picture appeared. After a dozen or so pictures had been viewed, Ellie could only say, "Amazing."

Ellie continued to look at Emmy's pictures as if each was a perfect portrait in all aspects. Emmy had created an entire series of masterpieces. What flabbergasted Ellie is that her much younger companion, someone who was young enough to be her daughter, had taken exposure after exposure while the truck was bouncing almost out of control. There were times when Ellie had to hold her own camera to keep it from being jarred out of her hands and falling out of the truck's open window. Ellie continued to view the next several pictures, her eyes leaving each to focus on Emmy as if to ask, "How did you do that?" Before she could really ask, there was a knock on the door and Luck and Far announced in unison, "You come. Eat."

The dining room chatter increased as several platters of Bickie's famous chicken were past around the table along with a dish that looked liked and vaguely tasted like mashed potatoes and another bowl with Bickie's homemade gravy and several native woven baskets filled with her biscuits. Luck and Fry had not forgotten the bowls of homemade jam and churned butter made with goat's milk. Joking and laughter knew no bounds the topics ranging from Mister Mar's new cast to Emmy falling off the truck onto the rhino's cage.

"How's it feel?" asked Bomba to Mister Mar as he raised his right leg out from the table and pointed at it. "You gonna live?"

Mister Mar gave a wry smile but was cut off by Mister Buster who said, "He'll live as long as Nurse Annemarie gives him his dose of TLC."

Everyone at the table laughed except Emmy who gave a questioning look to Ellie who was sitting next to her.

"Tender loving care," whispered Ellie.

Topics continued to jump from one member of the crew to another and ranged from what the next hunt would be to the trip into town the next day to drop off the rhino for shipment to somewhere in Germany. Tab, Jean Claude, Howdy and even Ellie became the brunt of various jokes going around the table. Emmy felt relieved that no one made fun of her. That relief was short lived. She didn't notice Mister Buster leave his seat and sneak up behind her. Before she realized, Buster had grabbed her by the shoulders and shouted, "Boo!" Emmy jumped straight up almost falling off her chair. Then she heard Buster say, "It's a good thing that old Mister Rhino has terrible vision," he started out, "or you, little Miss Picture Taker would have been feeling that nasty horn." He rubbed at his stomach. "You would've made a nice snack for him."

"Oh, Buster, stop it," said Ellie putting her arm around Emmy's shoulder. "You know that rhino's are vegetarians." She gave Emmy a gentle hug. "Don't listen to him," she said a sense of pride appearing on her face. "He doesn't know that he's in the presence of an artistic genius."

"Oh, stop patting yourself on the back, Ellie," said Buster.

"Not me," said Ellie pointing at Emmy. "This young lady took some of the finest pictures of our capture today that I've ever seen." She smiled at Buster. "She even made you look like a he-man great white hunter."

Laughter echoed from the table but all Emmy wanted to do was start crying again.

"When do we get to see these pictures?" asked Mister Mar as the others nodded, their expressions silently asking the same question.

The question went unanswered as Bickie came into the dining room and stopped by Mister Mar's chair. "You *irabiyoto?*" she asked.

"I'm definitely okay," he said giving a smile to Annemarie. "Are you okay?" he asked Bickie.

"*Aay-e,*" replied Bickie. "Is *emunyu aiya?*"

Mister Mar looked quickly around the table.

"The rhino's okay," answered Mister Bomba. He started grinning. "And so is old Tab here when he found out he didn't have to play matador." The table erupted in laughter.

"Tell me, Bickie," said Mister Mar, "what was in those two white things you gave to our nasty friend to calm him down."

"Bickie's bickies have mchicha and makande," she said seriously. "He sleep tonight."

Bickie turned and nodded for Luck and Far to join her in removing the bowls and platters from the table before they served dessert. Bickie didn't tell the rest of the table and didn't tell Mister Mar because he already knew, that she had laced the two biscuits with a ground root she had taken from her garden, the root a drug that was like a powered form of ether.

"Your pictures better be darned good the way Ellie is telling us young lady," said Mister Mar looking way too serious at Emmy. "If they're not, the next time I'm going to leave you on top of that cage."

Everyone at the table laughed except Emmy. She started crying.

"Nice goin', Mister Sensitive," said Annemarie as Ellie pulled Emmy to her so that Emmy's face was gently buried into her shoulder.

When dinner had finally ended and the table was clear, Mister Mar gave a nod to Ellie. She was up from the table with Emmy clutching to her side as she walked to the head of the table. "You push this button right here," she said indicating how to view Emmy's pictures.

"Hmmm," muttered Mister Mar as he looked seriously at Emmy. "Do you think you're good enough to be a part of this here crew?" he asked

"Oh, Mar," murmured Annemarie. "Look who you're talking to."

"I know who I'm talking to," he replied sternly. "Well, are you good enough?"

Emmy pulled away from Ellie and walked to where Mister Mar was sitting. She stood looking into his serious eyes that almost camouflaged a smile and took her Rebel out of his hands and began pushing the button to show him the pictures she had taken that day.

Dozens of pictures raced by Mister Mar's eyes before his hand went out and clamped down on Emmy's. "Missy, you're more than good enough." He released his hand and gestured to the others to gather around him. "Okay, Missy, show this group of societal misfits what you just showed me."

Emmy waited until everyone could see and then she started showing her pictures. Then entire show would've taken but an hour but she was interrupted countless times by questions and commands to go back and repeat a picture.

"Whoa there," said Howdy. "Is that me?"

"That's you the way I see you through my camera," Emmy said boldly as if she had been one of the crew her entire life.

"Cool," said Howdy.

There were more replies of, "Cool" as the camera continued to click away.

Annemarie let out several, "Oh, my," replies.

There were more than a few, "Darn, kid, you're good," comments that came from the men. Luck and Far, who had snuck back into the dining room giggled when they saw their images. Bickie did not giggle when she saw the series of photos depicting her encounter with the rhino. "Strong magic," she said to Emmy putting her hand on Emmy's shoulder, her eyes focused on the camera. "Bickie's stronger."

It seemed that the photo session would go on all night when Mister Mar's voice boomed out. "Big day tomorrow, ladies and gentlemen," he said. "Mister Rhino's going to town along with our lady zebra."

Ellie accompanied Emmy to her tiny room. As Emmy took off her hiking boots and outdoor clothes Ellie continue to examine her pictures more closely. "Amazing," she said to herself over and over again as the pictures marched by. "What an incredible talent."

Chapter 8

Emmy didn't have much trouble falling asleep. The excitement of the day had worn her out. Anticipating what would take place the next day, the new adventures, the sights and sounds propelled her into a dream world.

After breakfast she quickly discovered that she hadn't been dreaming as the crew loaded the rhinoceros onto Jean Claude's truck and the zebra on to Annemarie's smaller ambulance truck. This was going to be a different kind of trip Emmy quickly surmised the moment she saw Bomba, Howdy, Tab and Buster carrying large rifles as they got into their vehicles. Her facial expressions asked the question that Ellie, sitting next to her, answered without hesitating.

"Those are for protection against poachers."

"Poachers?" asked Emmy looking for clarification.

"Bad men who want to kill or steal animals for the ivory that are a part of them," said Ellie without taking her eyes off of Emmy. "Our rhino's horn is most valuable to some sad, sick people in the world."

"But, why?" asked Emmy in all innocence.

"Why indeed," said Ellie as the trucks started up and headed in an opposite direction than the day before. "It's called greed, Emmy. Some people will do anything for money." She paused and gave Emmy a serious look. "There are even some people, sick in their hearts and souls who will pay money to people like poachers to satisfy their sickness. They don't care who or what they harm as long as they get what they want."

"Is that why the men are carrying rifles today?"

"That would be my guess," said Ellie as she put her arm around Emmy's shoulder. "Are you sure you still want to go?"

Emmy nodded and climbed into the back of the truck, her harness on in an instant.

Emmy, her creative mind's eye whirling in high gear, did not lack for want of subjects to photograph as the small convoy of trucks carrying a rhinoceros and a zebra that would eventually be delivered to two different zoos in Europe plodded cautiously along. Emmy thought she remembered hearing that one zoo was located in Berlin, Germany. She had time to wonder about when the big order for a zoo in the Chicago area would be filled out, the order made in a conversation with Mister Mar by a Walt Waveland. Emmy wondered if that could be her father. She also wondered if Mister Mar really meant what he said about her being a part of the crew.

There were no signs of poachers during the trip. The convoy rumbled into the crowded streets of the small city. Emmy had no idea where she was. She had been so busy taking pictures of the new sights and scenes that she totally missed the sign with the city's name. The trucks had stopped in what looked like a freight yard. There was a single railroad track with several box cars coupled together. There were other trucks lined up, and it appeared that the rhinoceros and the zebra weren't the only animals destined to be taken out of Africa. Emmy saw Mister Mar disappear into a large dilapidated brick building. Emmy continued to take pictures and was about to unbuckle her harness when Mister Mar came out of the office with several men. They were all laughing. Mister Mar limped along with them and gave a hand and arm movement to the drivers of the trucks pointing in the direction where they should head to deliver the rhino. Mister Mar pointed at the truck that was carrying the zebra and it went toward the front of the train cars. The rhino headed for the next to the last car in line. The end car, a flat bed, had armor plated sides rising up and was armed with large weapons. Several men looking like soldiers were milling around by the car smoking.

Emmy had an unimpeded view of the train cars. She knew better than to get out of the truck even though the urge was overwhelming. Her telephoto lens went into action and so did her talent for the unique. Her eye caught Mister Mar talking to one of the men he had walked out of the building with. His face was void of emotion. Emmy's finger clicked the shutter. She wondered what Mister Mar's conversation had been about that had turned his face into a blank slate. There were many sides to Mister Mar that she had seen since she entered the compound with Bickie. She had not experienced this side of him. Emmy panned the train cars and got pictures of Jean Claude, Bomba and Howdy assisting some of the men who had exited the building with Mister Mar. They were loading the zebra into one freight car. At the other end, Emmy's telephoto lens saw the Maasai, Tab and Buster being assisted by several other men from the freight company carefully loading the rhinoceros in the last car. The men were straining with the weight of rhino and the cage. Muscles bulged from necks and arms. Leg muscles flexed from the short pants that all of the men wore. Emmy concentrated on the men's faces. Then something caught her attention. Her lens stopped on Mister Buster's face. Something clicked inside her and it wasn't a shutter. Her camera jumped to Mister Tab. There was another click. The lens went back forth several times and then Emmy knew where she had seen Mister Buster and Mister Tab before.

"They're movie stars," she said to an empty truck, Ellie having left to finish her photo assignment for CROW. Emmy's mind whirled. Mister Buster resembled another old movie star from the black and white movies Emmy had seen on television. His name was Buster Crabb and he was in several action films that she had watched. Mister Tab, on the other hand, she had seen in old color films on television, the station specializing in classic movies. He was Tab Hunter. Emmy thought he was kind of cute but not the way the announcer of the movie channel had stated saying that he was a heart throb and a handsome leading man.

Emmy had rested her Rebel in her lap. That's when she noticed Mister Mar heading in her direction. His blank look had changed to serious. He stopped and looked into the open window of the back seat where Emmy was sitting.

"Missy," he said sternly, I've notified the Tanganyika authorities and they're going to try and find out exactly where you came from and, hopefully, who and where your parents are so we can get you home."

"Thank you, Mister Mar," said Emmy and then tears

streamed down her cheeks.

"No need for the tears, Missy," said Mister Mar leaning inside the truck through the open window. "Anyone who can escape from a very angry rhino, get saved from hungry crocodiles by Bickie and stare down Big Bo shouldn't be crying.

"I miss my mom and dad," Emmy managed to sputter through her sniffles. "But I don't know if I'll ever see you and Bickie and Granna Ellie and the others again." Her tears flowed harder.

"You're not leaving us just yet," said Mister Mar. "You might be with us a week or so until the authorities can connect you with your parents." He gave Emmy a questioning look. "Did I hear you say something about a Granna Ellie?"

Emmy's hands rubbed the tears away from her eyes and off her cheeks. "I call Ellie, Mam," she said trying not to choke on her tears. "Sometimes it comes out sounding like, Gram."

"Well, Missy, if you want to call me Gramps, I won't mind," he said as a smile replaced his somber expression. "Just consider yourself one of the guys," he said, the smile growing. "But, first, you'd better dry those pretty eyes of yours. That is, if you want to be one of the guys."

Emmy lunged at Mister Mar catching him off guard. Her arms were around his neck and she gave him a hug. "Oh, Mister Mar," she said her arms not letting go. "You are awesome and I love you."

Ellie had witnessed the scene between Mister Mar and Emmy as she had walked toward the truck after finishing taking pictures. She looked in the open back window from her side of the truck. "Break it up you two," she said with a smile. "We don't want Annemarie to get jealous now do we?"

Business had been transacted—the most boring part of the trip to Emmy. She had finished taking some close up pictures of the soldiers at the end of the train. Miss Ellie had explained to her that they were guarding the train from being hijacked by poachers.

The trucks rumbled slowly out of the city the same way they had entered. Not one rifle made an appearance nor did anything resembling a poacher. As the trucks inched their way along one of the narrow streets crowded with shoppers milling around the open air bazaars, Emmy's heart skipped a beat. Her head jerked back over her shoulder and she muttered, "Mommy." She thought she had seen a woman who looked like her mother. There were three boys with the woman who resembled Emmy's brother. Before Emmy could get a better look the woman and the boys got swallowed up in the crowd.

"What was that you said?" asked Ellie.

"I thought I saw someone in the crowd back there that looked like my mother," she said cautiously. "My three brothers too."

"Jean Claude," said Ellie as she reached forward and put her hand on the driver's shoulder.

At the same time Emmy's own hand landed on Ellie's arm. "It' okay," she said. "It couldn't have been my mother. She's in Florida at Disney World looking for me."

"Are you sure you don't want to go back and look?"

"I'm sure," said Emmy not knowing what she was feeling

besides confused. She missed her family, but she had become so attached to this new group of adult friends along with Far and Luck that she dreaded the thought of having to leave them to go back home.

As the trucks lumbered along in the direction of the compound, Emmy felt bored. For the first time since finding herself half in and half out of the muck of the river bank, her nervous excitement had disappeared. She set her Rebel in her lap and gazed out the open window of the truck. Once again, the warm Serengeti air was putting a euphoric spell on her. She felt the relaxing breeze blowing across her face and soon her eye lids became heavy and she was dozing. A dream about her family soon materialized. The dream started out with Emmy's mother, father and her brothers all wearing big smiles. They were in a palm tree shaded garden surrounded by walls of flowers with blinding colors so beautiful that everyone around her was squinting. Then the walls of flowers seemed to grow, slowly bending over them like a giant roof. Before Emmy realized soldiers entered into the garden. They were the same soldiers who she saw standing by the last train car in the freight yard. The soldiers pointed their rifles at her parents and began herding them into a compound that was identical to the one where she had been staying. Her parents and brothers walked obediently into a pen like she had seen the rhinoceros and zebra locked up the day before. Inside the pen were Bickie, Luck and Far. They had been forced into the pen earlier and were kneeling with their hands tied behind them. Other armed men were inside the pen. They were dressed partially in raggedy looking military uniforms covering torn, filthy t-shirts. One of the shirts had a badly stained image of Mickey Mouse. The men looked beyond raggedy. They also looked mean and were carrying guns, different guns than the rifles she saw being carried by Bomba, Howdy, Tab and Buster before they had left to deliver the rhinoceros and the zebra. Instantly she knew the guns were automatic weapons designed to kill people. There had been too many news clips on television showing those guns and Emmy knew the men using them could kill many people in seconds.

The truck in her dream pulled up to the open gate of the pen and Emmy was out the back door and heading toward the pen, her Rebel in hand. "Leave my mommy alone!" she shouted. She raised her Rebel, snapped several pictures then lowered her camera. "Take that!" she hollered out. "You'll be sorry!" she continued to shout. "I know where you live."

The mean raggedy men either didn't hear her or were ignoring her because of her size.

Emmy found herself standing at the front of the gate which somehow was locked. She looked through the wire at her family. They were kneeling alongside Bickie, Luck and Far, their heads down and their hands tied behind their back. The raggedy looking men were in an animated argument. One pointed his weapon at the kneeling group and took it away when another of his comrades yelled something at him. Another man motioned his right hand across his throat.

"No!" Emmy screamed in a shrill voice.

Again, the men appeared not to hear her.

Emmy could see two of the men standing at the entrance to the dining room. Each had a large red can in his hand and they were pouring liquid out of their cans and laughing as they watched it splash on the wooden porch and steps. Liquid found the walls and Emmy watched it run down to the porch floor.

The pouring and splashing didn't last long. Emmy saw both men toss their cans aside and then reach into their respective pockets of the tattered military style jackets they were wearing and pull out a small object. She didn't have to wait long to see that the small object was a book of matches. Those match books turned into flame and then were nonchalantly tossed on the porch. Emmy choked as she saw the main building become engulfed in flames.

"Why?"Emmy screamed again as she watched the two men backing away, big grins on their dark, scarred faces. They turned and walked back to the pen as if nothing had happened.

Emmy felt helpless. She could feel anger building; this wasn't the same anger she would unleash when her brothers would pick on her. This new feeling was more intense and it frightened her. Emmy had never felt revenge before and now she wanted to get back at the men who had destroyed the compound. "I'm going to make you pay for what you did to Mister Mar's house," she said as she found herself running at full speed toward the two men, her camera strap around her neck. She barreled head on into the two only she didn't hit them. She ran right through them as if they were ghosts. She stopped, turned and looked at the men. They didn't notice her and walked into the pen. Then she heard Bickie.

"Be calm, Missy."

Emmy looked at Bickie and saw a slight knowing smile.

"It's okay," Emmy heard Bickie say but it didn't sound like Bickie's voice. Then she felt something on her arm. She blinked. "It's okay." She blinked again and saw Ellie, her comforting eyes smiling at her.

"It looks like you were having a bad dream," said Ellie.

Emmy soon discovered that her bad dream wasn't as bad as what happened next. It was worse.

The convoy had just made the final turn in the rut road that led to the front of the compound when each truck came to a quick stop. The vehicles all seemed to freeze in place at once, each ending up in a line stretching across the front of the compound. No one got out. No one moved. They only looked. What they saw was faint black smoke coming from a charred frame skeleton that used to be the compound. The only recognizable thing standing was a portion of what used to be Bickie's kitchen. There were no signs of Bickie, Luck and Far. The remains of the animals that had been in the compound were all that was left. They were now carcasses and in no need of being treated by Annemarie.

Mister Mar was the first out of the truck, the cast on his leg making his exit a bit clumsy. He was joined by Howdy, Buster, Tab and Bomba. The four Maasai men who had accompanied them to help with the delivery joined the others as did Annemarie and Jean Claude. Ellie sat in the truck with Emmy in silence, each trying to comprehend what happened.

Click, click, click, click went the shutter to Emmy's Rebel. Then her door opened and she was out of the truck walking toward the others, her camera covering her face. Click, click, click. Suddenly she stopped taking pictures. Her heart also seemed to stop. She was standing next to Mister Mar in the open gate to the pen. The grotesque scene in front of her sent her to her knees. Luck and Far were lying among the remains of the animals. They too were carcasses in no need of being treated by Annemarie. Emmy's head turned and she looked up at Mister Mar, tears in her eyes. "Why, Mister Mar?" she asked.

Mister Mar never said a word and didn't look down at Emmy. He placed his hand gently on her head.

"But, why?" asked Emmy, her question choked.

"Don't know, Missy," replied Mister Mar, his voice soft and calm. "But we'll find out."

Emmy felt Mister Mar shift his weight and turn to where Bomba, Howdy, Tab and Buster were standing. She could see that they didn't believe what they were seeing. Emmy knew that Mister Mar had given the men a sign because they quickly headed back to their respective trucks. In less than a minute, they were back inside the pen each carrying what she later learned was a canvas tarpaulin. She felt Mister Mar's hand drop to her shoulder and he gave a gentle pressure indicating that she should head back to the truck. "They were my friends too," said Emmy to Mister Mar who was several steps in front of her.

Ellie and Annemarie were next to Emmy and joined her as she followed just behind Mister Mar and the four men carrying the tarps. "Emmy," said Ellie softly. "Are you sure you don't want to go back to the truck?"

Emmy's head went once to the left and then to the right. "They were my friends too," she repeated with compassion as hear tears welled up and dropped down her cheeks.

The scene inside the pen went beyond gruesome. Luck and Far had been brutally murdered. Ellie, Annemarie and the men also knew that they had been tortured and molested by at least five poachers dressed in tattered military uniforms. Emmy didn't quite comprehend that the men responsible for the deaths of Luck and Far were also dead. They were all kneeling, hands stretched out as if pleading with looks of fear plastered across their faces. Each body looked like it had turned to stone.

Emmy watched as Bomba, Howdy, Tab and Buster with the assistance of Annemarie, placed the tarpaulins over the bodies of the two dead girls. The four Maasai men stood silent and motionless just inside the open gate.   Then Emmy heard murmuring and she along with the others turned to see Bickie emerge from the still smoking ruins of what was once her kitchen. Draped around her shoulders hanging lifeless was Big Bo her pet rock python.   Emmy saw that the snake looked different and didn't realize how different until she noticed the snake's head was gone.

Bickie walked slowly up to Mister Mar and stopped to face him. Her eyes were sad and she looked as if she had been crying. "By time I get to dem," she said her words coming out slowly and filled with pain, "dey dead."

Mister Mar didn't say a word, his head going up and down once in a nod.

"I try save," Bickie managed to say.

The sadness on Mister Mar's face was joined by a single

blink as the others stood by, respective looks of disbelief and grief at what they were witnessing.

"Bickie make dem pay," she said an anger spreading across her face. "Dey pays for hurting my babies."

Emmy didn't' realize that what she smelled was death. The others knew. Life in the Serengeti had taught each of them that lesson.

Mister Mar looked at Bickie and said softly, "Bickie, ask the Maasai men how they want to handle the burial of their two young women."

Bickie didn't give any indication that she heard Mister Mar's request. Her attention seemed to be focused off to the right of the compound's ruins at the corner of where the path to her garden started.

Emmy had also seen the movement.

Bickie slowly walked over to the covered remains of Far and Luck and gently placed Big Bo alongside of the two girls. She murmured something that only Emmy heard but didn't understand. Then she turned and stood perfectly still. Everyone could see where her eyes were focused.

Emmy saw Mister Mar start to take a step with Bomba, Howdy, Tab and Buster about to follow. Then she saw Bickie's hand go up like a shot as if she were a police officer stopping traffic. The men stopped. No one moved. Emmy, both of her hands holding her Rebel just above waist high, watched Bickie. She wasn't moving either. Then she heard Bickie's murmuring turn into a chant. Emmy didn't know what Bickie was chanting. The only ones in the group who did know were the Maasai men and they kept their distance, not moving, standing by the covered remains of Far and Luck.

Bickie started to walk where she had seen the undergrowth at the edge of the path move. As she walked, she kept staring at the spot, her chants getting louder and her eyes turning a fiery red.

Emmy saw Bickie get within several strides of the path when the jungle seemed to erupt. Out jumped a man dressed identical to five dead others in the pen. He started down the path trying to run at full speed, but as hard as he tried and as fast as his legs moved, he was barely going as fast as a snail.

Bomba, Howdy, Tab and Buster started after the man but stopped as if each had collided head on with the giant Umbrella Thorn Acacia tree that stood majestically in the front yard of the compound. They watched as Bickie kept getting nearer the raggedy looking soldier. Even from where they were standing they all could see the look of fear and impending doom plastered on the man's face. He was going to die like his comrades and he knew it. He also knew that having watched them die, his death would be worse. It would be worse because he was the one that instigated the abuse and molesting of Far and Luck, indicating to the others that they should also have their turn as well. He had seen Bickie's rock python and wanted a trophy—the valuable skin of the snake that would bring him at least a year's wages paid by some Oriental collector. What the soldier hadn't seen was Bickie. She had been on her way back from collecting vegetables for a special dinner to celebrate the delivery of the rhino and the zebra. She had smelled the faint aroma of smoke as far away as her garden. That's when she had quickened her pace. She went as fast as she could on her one good foot and went even faster when she heard the cries of Luck and Far.

Bickie had wasted no time when she got back to the compound. The building was an inferno and her two girls lie motionless on the ground in front of the gluttonous fire devouring everything on its menu.

Five soldiers couldn't believe their eyes. Here was a crippled old woman coming directly at them. She had a hobbled skip-like stride. They looked at one another and started laughing. While they laughed and picked up their guns to dispatch the old woman into the hereafter, their leader was taking a machete to a prized rock python. All six had experienced their own drug induced states of euphoria enhanced by the money they would receive for their handiwork. Then everything changed.

The five soldiers' guns were at the ready, fingers on the respective triggers. There was only one problem. As hard as they tried to fire their weapons aimed at Bickie, they found their fingers wouldn't work. They couldn't squeeze the triggers. Blank looks replaced levity and that's when they noticed the blazing red of the old woman's eyes and heard the roar of her chant.

A sixth renegade poacher stood out of sight behind the back of the smoldering building. He was almost drooling as he admired his new prize. In his shaking hands was the body of a headless Big Bo. He had just kicked away the snake's severed head and was ready to remove the skin, his trophy, from the snake's still tense body. To his surprise he found he could barely move. Then he heard screams and they were not those of the two girls. His men were screaming. The snake slithered out of his weak hands and lay at his feet in a coil. At that point, the soldier felt only one thing. Survival. He left the dead snake and managed to stagger to the edge of the building that had been spared by the fire. One eye peered around the corner and caught a glimpse of what was happening. A glimpse was too much. He somehow pulled his head back out of sight. One thought raced through his mind. He knew what he had to do. He knew what he wanted to do. Getting away was that one thing; the saving of his own life from the fate that had his five comrades pleading and screaming for their lives. All he could do was to try and avoid the same fate that the five others were meeting. The frightened poacher saw the rock python still coiled up as if waiting for him to get within striking distance. The prized skin that was to make him a rich man was now traded for the will to live.

Screams that had caused animals to scatter across the plains of the Serengeti were soon reduced to whimpers. Then silence followed. The poacher's will to live kicked in, but that was all that kicked in. He found it too hard and cumbersome to walk and running was out of the question. His legs felt like stone. He got down on his hands and knees and began to crawl to the opening of a path he saw at the edge of the jungle. If he could make that path he thought, he would live. He would be safe in the jungle thicket surrounded by Sausage trees, the gnarled, tangled roots of Strangler Figs, Toothbrush trees and Whistling Thorns even if the thorn trees were filled with biting ants at the base of their trunks. He continued to crawl on his belly toward the jungle underbrush as if he had become the rock python. His survival instinct kept him going. If he could conceal himself in the thick cover, he thought, he could formulate a plan to escape. When he first started crawling, the pleas of the other poachers were deafening. Then the screams had turned to whimpers and whispered pleas coated with tears. Now the only thing he heard was his own breathing; that and what sound like a chant coming from the crippled woman. From where he was hiding in the jungle the poacher had a perfect view of the old woman and his five cohorts. The five, he knew, were dead. What almost scared the sole survivor to death was that his men looked as if they had been turned into stone. He saw five monuments kneeling not too far from the two dead girls as if asking for their forgiveness. None came.

The surviving poacher began to understand that his time was near. The old woman was now looking in his direction and had started limping towards him. She appeared in no hurry. It was if she were toying with him, taunting him, the same way he did Far and Luck and same way he did to Bickie's pet rock python.

Mister Mar and his four crew members, with Annemarie trailing, started following Bickie. They watched as she went around a turn in the path and disappeared from their view. The cast on Mister Mar's legs made him walk exactly like Bickie. That didn't seem to slow him down.

"Come on, Ellie," said Emmy as if ordering her much older friend. "We've got to help Bickie. I think that bad man has a gun." She grabbed Ellie's hand and started running after Mister Mar and the others who had just disappeared from view after entering the opening to the jungle path. "I've got to be there for Bickie," she said pulling a stumbling Ellie behind her.

Neither Emmy nor Ellie had any idea of how they could help Bickie against a ruthless poacher armed with a gun. All they knew is that they wanted to help and somehow they would.

Mister Mar and his crew slapped aside palm branches as

they followed several turns in the path. Then they saw Bickie. She had caught up to the man. Actually, catching up to him wasn't that difficult. He had gone from a crawl to a stooped over walk once he had gotten out of undercover in the jungle. That didn't last long. Soon he resembled and infant who had discovered that balance was part of walking. He had dropped to his knees and was barely able to crawl. When Mister Mar and the others saw Bickie and the man he was continually looking back over his shoulder. The look of incredible agony was written all over his face. Bickie slowly hobbled to the man, stopped and pointed at him with her two extended index fingers; her thumbs pointed down. Her chanting was barely audible but at a frenzy.

Emmy, Ellie and Annemarie stood together, arms around each other's shoulders and didn't say a word. Neither did Mister Mar and the others. They watched in silence and wished they hadn't. Bickie's chants, the man's screams and pleas and a cluster of crocodiles splashing in the shallows of the river below them was enough to chill their blood. At least their blood didn't turn to stone. The poacher soon ended up like his colleagues, frozen for all eternity in a lifeless monument. He knelt, arms out, eyes pleading, an open mouth begging but no words coming out. Stone can't speak.

Emmy, the shutter bug, somehow fired off rapid sequence after rapid sequence of what had transpired. She was totally focused on her camera. Right near the end, she got frustrated because the memory card in her camera had filled up. Her frustration grew because her good luck charm in her pants pockets had never felt so hot. She thought she was being set on fire like the compound. Ignoring the burning sensation, Emmy reached into her shoulder bag and frantically searched for a spare memory chip for her camera. Her other hand had popped out the full memory card and she stuffed that in her pocket with her good luck charm. "Oh, darn," she said feeling frustrated because she couldn't find any of her spare memory cards. She gave her shoulder bag a vicious shake and started to drop to a knee to give her better support. Her foot slipped from where she had been standing on the edge of the path not realizing the river was below her down a steep embankment. She tried to cry out for help but she was tumbling out of control down the hill toward the river. At the river's edge were the crocodiles.

Chapter 9

Emmy thought she saw shapes through the churning current of the river. The shapes were a blurred white. Her name was being called out, but it was in a whisper. It reminded her of the sound the wind had made when it hit the side of their Land Rover and bringing an end to the family safari to Disney World. The shapes above the churning current became crystal clear. They were two baby elephants. Only these elephants were pink. Emmy found herself sandwiched between the two elephants and hugging one with her right arm and the other with her left. "Oh, I missed you guys so much," she said, her voice full of love and cheer.

"Emma Grace," a familiar voice whispered to her. "Emma Grace."

She tried to move, to open her eyes, but the stuffed pink elephants had their trunks covering her face and mouth, almost suffocating her. Her fingers traced the elephant's trunks and she wanted to laugh. Nothing came out.

"Hey, Emmy Lou," another voice said, this one deeper than the other.

"Mister Mar," she murmured. "Is that you?"

"She's awake," the familiar voice said sounding relieved. "Our baby's awake."

"Baby?" repeated Emmy, swatting at the elephants' trunks,

the churning current of the river turning calm, serene and crystal clear. "I'm Emma Waveland," she heard herself mutter sounding defiant. "I'm not a baby. Babies don't photograph wild animals with their Granna Ellie. Babies don't have Maasai friends like Luck and Far. Babies don't make biscuits with Bickie. She began to giggle and reached for the elephants' trunks. They weren't there. She tried to sit up. "I'm not a baby," she said again, this time more authoritarian.

"Emma, it's your mother," the familiar voice said.

Emmy sat up in the hospital bed. Her head ached and she knew there was a bandage that went around her forehead. She was confused as she saw her mother, father and brothers all sitting around her bed. They all tried to tell her at once how lucky she had been that the safari driver, Jean Claude had pulled her out of the river after she had accidentally fallen out of the Land Rover while trying to take a picture when the storm hit.

Emmy didn't remember.

"We're all so thankful you're safe," said her mother holding both of Emmy's hands in her own. "We will always be eternally grateful to Jean Claude for how fast he got you out of that river."

"Yep," her father said. "Those Disney folks sure know how to train their people to handle any situation." His head went slowly from side to side. "You took quite a tumble down that embankment," he said, his head now going slowly up and down. "I hope you learned your lesson about not leaning out of an open air truck so far that you fell out."

"Yeah," replied her brother, Josh with a big grin mocking her. "You should have seen the neat series of rolls you took down that hill. Scott and Todd never did that many the time we went to the Indiana Dunes.

Emmy looked at her parents and brothers as if she didn't know what they were talking about. "It wasn't Jean Claude who saved me from the river and the crocodiles," she started to explain before being cut off by her father.

"Emma, there are no crocodiles in that man-made river you tumbled into because you got careless," her father stated.

"But, Daddy," she said, cutting him off. "There were crocodiles. I saw them. I saw what they did to Bickie's foot."

"Bickie?" both her parents asked at the same time, puzzled looks on their faces as well as those of her brothers.

"Bickie saved me," said Emmy, looking into her mother's questioning eyes. She introduced me to Mister Mar and Miss Annemarie and my new friends, Far and Luck." She could see the looks of doubt on the faces of her family and also those of who she thought were a doctor and two nurses in the room. Emmy's hands formed into fists. She wasn't angry only frustrated. Her brothers' behaviors irritated her, but that was something she expected from them; acting sympathetic and caring while trying to hide their grins, not believing a word their sister said. "You don't believe me, do you?" stated Emmy. Then she started to cry. "But I can prove what happened. I have the pictures." She became almost frantic and tried to get out of the hospital bed, the tray table blocking her way. "My camera bag," she said, looking as if she were in a state of panic.

"Where's my camera bag? Where's my Rebel? Where's my iPhone. I have the pictures."

Walt Waveland glanced over to the doctor. "How hard did she hit her head when she took a tumble out of that Land Rover during the freak storm?" he asked.

The doctor appeared understanding. He smiled at Emmy while talking to her parents. "That's hard to tell," he said. "Our initial test showed only a slight concussion; that and the bump on her head and the scrapes on her elbows and knees.

"But Miss Annemarie, she was the one who gave me first aid and took care of me after Bickie pulled me from that yucky river bank." Her eyes were pleading with her parents to believe her. "I have the pictures," she said partially choking on her words. "I can prove all of it. Just get me my camera bag. I know I had it when I slipped and rolled down that hill into the river. I know I had it," she said, as tears trickled down her cheeks.

Walt Waveland gently stroked his daughter's right cheek with the back of his fingers. "Honey," he said using a rare name for his daughter that he did only in the most of serious situations. "I'm afraid your cameras and your iPhone got wet when you ended up in the river. Your bag got pulled out but it had been in the water for a long time while the paramedics were treating you. It was Josh who fished the bag out of the river.

"Thing must've had ten gallons of water in it," said Josh, his normal cocky self acting like he had been the one who saved his sister. "I bet none of that stuff of yours will work," he said, then stopped when he saw his father's look.

"Your cameras are drying out in our hotel room back at the Palms," said her father. "Your mother rode in the ambulance with you to the hospital and I took your brothers in the van to the hotel to get you some dry clothing before we came here." He paused. "Todd and Scott put your cameras on the balcony table to dry out."

What about my memory cards?" Emmy asked, her head pounding and the tears flowing. "There were at least three in one of the side pockets of my bag and a new one in the Rebel. I was trying to put it in when I slipped and fell." The back of Emmy's hand wiped her eyes. "My shorts," she almost shouted. "Where are my shorts?" She glanced around the hospital room. "I put a memory card in my pocket. It had pictures of Bickie and the poachers." She began to sob. "I had pictures of my dead friends and...." She looked at everyone in the room but could see the doubt. She chocked back her sobs and managed to say, "Bickie even took a Selfie."

"You can check on your memory cards when you get back to the hotel," her father said. Then he forced a smile. "The doctor said you can get out of the hospital this afternoon if you feel up to it."

"But my hiking shorts?" she asked.

"They're hanging in the closet with your other belongings," said one of the nurses. She took Emma's hiking shorts out and handed them to her.

Emmy's thrust her hand into one of the pockets almost putting a hole in the fabric. She felt nothing. Her hand now fumbled into the next pocket. Nothing. Three became the lucky number. Her heart seemed to miss several beats as she slowly removed the memory card and held it in between her thumb and forefinger. "I told you I can prove it." Sticking out from behind the memory card was her good luck charm.

The doctor had given Emmy the okay to leave the hospital after she had assured him that her headache had gone. It hadn't, but Emmy, ever the rebel, wanted to prove that the stories she told her parents about what had happened to her when she was in the real Africa actually happened. The ride back to the hotel seemed to take forever and all the while Emmy kept hoping and praying that her pictures hadn't been destroyed.

As she entered their hotel room at the Palms, she saw her cameras lined up on a large white bath towel. They were on the table outside on the balcony sitting in the sunlight. Next to her cameras was her camera bag. Emmy carefully unzipped the side pocket of the bag and slid her fingers inside. Her face lit up and she removed three tiny memory chips. They were just as she remembered putting them. Next she slid open the tiny access door to the Camedia's card. She had only used that camera when she first arrived at the compound with Bickie, then it stayed in her bag. The card popped out and she removed it, blowing on what appeared to be traces of moisture. She repeated the process with her Rebel. "Where's my iPhone?" she asked politely, her eyes glancing around the room.

"It's next to you cameras," he father said. "That leopard skin design on it makes a nice contrast with the white towel, don't you think." Her father gave her a grain. "Did you get dat leopard when you were in Africa?"

"Thanks, Dad," Emmy said, ignoring her father's attempt at making a joke. She picked up her iPhone. "Do you think it'll work?"

Her father gave a shrug. "I don't know, Emmy Lou," he said. "Why don't you see if it'll take a charge, hey" he said. Then he quickly cautioned, "Be careful. You don't want that thing to explode in your hands.' He gave a shrug. "Tell you what, Emmy," he said reaching for her iPhone, "I'll plug it in for you."

The iPhone to everyone's surprise did what an iPhone was supposed to do when plugged into the charger cable. It began to charge. "Thank you, Daddy," Emmy said giving her father a hug. She quickly let go and began to dig into the contents of her duffle bag. "Here it is," she said holding up a small black box just slightly bigger than a match book. "I can plug this into my tablet and copy my pictures into my photo program." Her hands had the cable plugged into her tablet and one of the tiny memory cards was slid into a slot. "Oh, please work," she said, her words like a prayer. She held her breath, pushed a button and waited. "Oh, God," she said glancing at her father and then at her mother. "It's working," she said. "At least I think it works."

"At least it's not smoking or shooting out sparks," her father said.

"Oh, Walt."

"Well, it hasn't exploded and sent all of us flying over the balcony," Emmy's father said.

"Daddy, stop!" Emmy looked at the tablet screen and muttered. "The pictures I took of the animals are there. It works!"

"Are you sure those aren't the pictures you took while we were on safari?" he asked. "Those animals look like the same ones I saw."

Emmy appeared not to hear her father. Her fingers popped out the memory card and inserted another one. "This is from my Rebel." The card went in the slot and she pushed a button. Nothing happened. Emmy glanced at her father and then at the tablet. She exhaled and gave a relieved sigh. "The gosh darned plug came out," she said. Her fingers pushed the connector back in the slot and then she pushed the button again. "It works, Dad."

Picture upon picture transferred from the tiny memory card in seconds. Emmy couldn't believe her eyes.

Her father couldn't believe his eyes either. Then neither could her mother. Her brothers dropped their skepticism and moved closer. "Neat pick-up truck," Josh said. "I never saw a seat mounted on a front fender before."

"Yeah, you did," said Todd. "There was one of those seats in that movie that we watched about trapping animals for zoos on the way down here. Don't you remember?"

"Josh is too stupid to remember his name," added Scott.

"Oh, what do you know," snapped Josh. "You're the runt of the litter. You're so stupid you put on that batting helmet backwards when dad took us to that batting cage."

"I did not."

"Yeah, you did. You were so stupid that you didn't even know who that old guy was that dad got to give us batting tips."

"I did so."

"Stop it!" said Walt Waveland. The expression on his face added to his command for the argument between his sons to end. "For your enlightenment, your mother and I saw dat movie long before you three were born." He smiled at his sons. "That was a cool seat mounted on that fender. I bet ol' John

Wayne loved sitting on that seat chasing wild animals all over Africa."

Before any of her family could get a closer look at the pictures, Emmy had popped the memory card out and inserted the final one. The button was pushed and the process repeated. Now four heads almost totally blocked Emmy's view of the screen. Her heart sank. The pictures she had taken from the balcony on their first night in Florida flashed by; then there were exterior shots of the Wildlife Park itself and the empty Land Rover. Jean Claude's picture flashed by followed by the animals they had seen. The animals were real, just like the ones she remembered seeing on the Serengeti. Several blank spaces appeared and then there was the compound. Emmy started to cry.

It was her mother who comforted her and then suggested they all go down the street from their hotel to an old fashioned ice cream parlor. "I think we could all use a treat," said Betty Waveland. "The pictures can wait."

Ice cream didn't do a thing for Emmy. She had ordered a single dip vanilla cone and barely touched it while her brothers inhaled the biggest banana splits her parents had ever seen. Josh even said to Emmy after devouring his banana split: "Are you gonna finish your ice cream cone?"

Emmy barely shook her head and the ice cream cone was snatched from her hand and devoured by Josh.

When the family returned to the hotel and their room Emmy went to her iPhone. She unplugged the charger cord and turned on the phone. She almost fainted. The iPhone worked. "Oh, please be there," she said to the camera that was shaking in her hands. "Oh, dear God, please be there."

Emmy could barely see the images come alive on her iPhone through her tears, but they were there, life like, her friends from Africa. Bickie smiled at her. So did Luck and Far in their red shukas. Emmy wanted to hug them. There were pictures of Mister Mar and the other men of his crew: Mister Buster, Mister Tab, Mister Howdy and Mister Bomba hammed it up for her in front of her camera. There was a picture of Jean Claude. Miss Annemarie smiled at her as pictures jumped off the iPhone screen at her. Emmy pushed a button and the pictures started again. "Bickie's Selfie," she yelled out startling her parents. Several more pictures flashed by. Emmy's finger tip pressed and slid across the screen a picture stopping, proud knowing eyes looking back at her. "I'm so happy I got to meet you, Granna Ellie," said Emmy.

"Who?" her father asked. He stared at the picture of his late grandmother. "He looked at his daughter and then at his wife. "How did you get this?"

Emmy sat on the sofa in the living room of the hotel suite surrounded by her parents and brothers. She'd gone through the iPhone pictures several times, explaining and embellishing her explanations and being sure to highlight her encounter with the crocodiles.

"Stop it on dat picture," he father stated politely. He studied the picture on the screen. "Did you say this man's name was Mister Mar?"

Emmy gave a nod.

"Doesn't he look kind of familiar to you?" her father asked as he showed the picture to Emmy's mother. Before she could answer he returned the camera to his daughter. "And you said his name was Mister Mar?

Emmy nodded again. "He did tell me his real name once; said he hated his name."

"What was his name?" her father asked cautiously.

"His parents called him Marion Robert Morrison," said Emmy. "He didn't like being called, Marion so he cut it short to, Mar," explained Emmy to her father. "That's how he explained it to me one night after dinner in the compound's dining room."

Emmy's father let out a whistle as his head went from side to side. "You still don't see the resemblance of your Mister Mar and the man who played in the movie dat you and your brothers watched in the van on the way down here?"

"He did look kind of familiar now that I think of it," said Emmy. "He was such a nice man. Everyone in the compound was really nice." She let out a sigh and her eyes began to tear up. "I wonder if I'll ever get to see any of them again."

"So you think this Mister Mar fellow looked kind of familiar, did you?" he father repeated with a smile. "Emmy, did you ever hear of the late movie star, John Wayne?"

Epilogue

Emmy watched the movie on the way home. So did her brothers. Her mother also was in the back of the van watching John Wayne catch wild animals for a zoo. None of them could believe what they saw and none of them wanted to believe that what Emmy saw was the result of a bump on the head. She had too many pictures as proof of what had happened to her.

"Dad," said Josh as they were nearing the end of their vacation and was within several miles of their house. "Did you really know that old guy you introduced us to at the Atlanta Braves spring training ball park who worked with us on our batting?" he asked.

"Yep," came the reply from the front seat.

"Did he really hit 500 home runs in the majors?"

"He sure did."

"How come me and my brothers never heard of him?"

Walt Waveland laughed. "For the same reason you three needed batting tips."

"Dad, this isn't going to be one of your long, boring lectures is it?" asked Josh.

"Yeah, Dad," said Scott. "I'd rather be in church listening to some old priest talk about good and evil.

"I agree with Scott," said Todd. "At least in church I could sleep through the sermon."

Walt Waveland let out a laugh. "Let me tell you something, my three sons with the world's worst batting averages," he said. "The reason you never heard of dat gentleman who, by the way, is in the Hall of Fame, is because you three never listen. I don't think you know how to listen." He paused and then added, "The Baseball Hall of Fame I mentioned is in Cooperstown, New York. Maybe we can go there on our next vacation." He paused. No one saw his smile. "That is if our little Miss Shutter Bug promises not to fall down the stadium steps while taking pictures."

Emmy didn't laugh at her father's comment. Her three brothers were hilarious.

"Quiet back there," ordered their father. "If I may continue," he said. "The reason or reasons why you three bird brains never heard of dat Hall of Fame gentleman is dat first, you're members of the C and T."

"You're point," interrupted Josh. "What's this C and T stuff?"

"My point is dat if anyone in your generation ever took long enough to stop talking on those cell phones and crippling your thumbs with those text messages, you'd see my point. My point pertains to reading. It pertains to what I said about listening. If you did, you'd know all about who's in the Hall of Fame; you'd know about the history of the game you play. You'd know about the great hitters and how they got dat way," he said his sarcasm mounting. "Besides, you're all so darned lazy you want everything handed to you on a silver platter. Like every pitch in your wheelhouse." He paused and glanced in the rear view mirror, surprised to see that his sons were listening to him.

"Those are just a few of the reasons why you didn't know who Hank Aaron was." He laughed again. "Now take your little sister for example. "She knows the history of photography. She took the trouble to find that information out and she went through a lot of trouble to practice her craft." He paused to get the van off the center line of the highway. "Did you ever hear of practice makes perfect?" he asked his sons. He didn't give them time to answer. "Dat's a lot of bunk." He glanced in the rear view mirror. "Perfect practice makes perfect, gentlemen."

"Oh, Walt," said Betty Waveland. "Don't you think the boys have heard enough of your lecturing?"

"Not until the next time they strikeout."

Emmy never heard a word. Her eyes were glued to the television screen as the movie, *Hatari* moved along. She absorbed every scene that Mister Mar was in and looked desperately for the other crewmembers along with Bickie, Luck and Far. They weren't there. Neither was Granna Ellie. She thought she recognized Annemarie but wasn't sure. One thing she was positive of was the rhinoceros. He could have been a twin to the one she came face to horn with.

Emmy could feel her good luck charm warm and snug in the pocket of her hiking shorts. She turned on her iPhone. In seconds the screen lit up and Emmy smiled back at the picture of her Granna Ellie smiling back at her.

Title: The Dutchman's Gift

- Author: Richard Baran
- Publisher: TotalRecall Publications, Inc.
- Paperback, ISBN: 9781590952979
- Ebook, Nook, Kindle, ISBN: 9781590952986
- Number of pages: 124
- Publication Date: 2015

A twelve year old boy finds a magical Apache arrowhead while hiking with his grandfather in the Superstition Mountains of Arizona. The arrowhead transports the boy from a Disney World rollercoaster ride back over one hundred and fifty years to the Superstitions where he meets "The Lost Dutchman."

Title: Where Have All the Go-Go's Gone?

Part I

- Author: Richard Baran
- Publisher: TotalRecall Publications, Inc.
- Hard Cover, ISBN: 9781590952399
- Paperback, ISBN: 9781590952405
- Ebook, Nook, Kindle, ISBN: 9781590952412
- Number of pages: 304
- Publication Date: 2015

Bo Pepperwall's intelligence dwarfed Mensa's parameters. He was perceived as strange thereby resulting in his being ridiculed by many, shunned by most and being called, Bo the Schmoe by all. Then he faced a dilemma. He had to choose between money (which he never had) and morals (which he also lacked). Should he weasel a part of his recently widowed sister's inheritance for a business venture or should he turn in the killer of her husband, his despicable brother-in-law? He chooses both. Bo opens La Tinkerbelle's a Go-Go, a 1960's retro discotheque in an abandoned factory building in a Chicago slum using a theme from the legend of Peter Pan. Surrounding himself with bizarre employees (each having a unique vision of reality) who put fun into dysfunctional, his dream nearly goes bust. Then a Chicago gossip columnist prints a story that has customers lined up and Bo collides with his dilemma. The collision buries him in money and public adulation. Success, however, can't cover his moral guilt in the surprise ending to this murder mystery farce that is more farce than mystery.

Title: When Will They Ever Learn?

Part II

Where Have All the Go-Go's Gone?

- Author: Richard Baran
- Publisher: TotalRecall Publications, Inc.
- Hard Cover, ISBN: 9781590952429
- Paperback, ISBN: 9781590952436
- Ebook, Nook, Kindle, ISBN: 9781590952443
- Number of pages: 220
- Publication Date: 2015

Bo Pepperwall, a card carrying member of Mensa, dreamer, conniver and ridiculed lifelong loser opens *La Tinkerbelle's a Go-Go*. A 1960's retro discotheque located in a Chicago slum, he uses a theme from the legend of Peter Pan that includes a scantily clad Tinker Bell. He finances his business by weaseling part of his sister's inheritance away from her. He also witnesses the murder of his despicable brother-in-law, the mayor of Glen Forest on the Watercourse, a prestigious Chicago North Shore community. Bo, however, remains a loser and his garish disco faces bankruptcy until an article by a Chicago gossip columnist turns it into a bonanza. That same day, Tinker Bell's outraged mother accidentally sets fire to La Tinkerbelle's and destroys the booming business. Bo and his employees—along with two black cats named Heckle and Jeckle—end up in court charged with violations of the Mann Act; contributing to the delinquency of minors; ignoring EPA laws; cruelty to animals and presenting lewd and indecent performances. Bo turns in the killer and the court finds him innocent of the criminal charges in the surprise ending to this murder mystery zany comedy.

Title: The Jacket

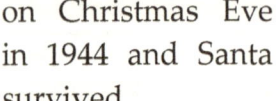

- Author: Richard Baran
- Publisher: TotalRecall Publications, Inc.
- Hard Cover ISBN: 9781590955659
- Paperback, ISBN: 9781590955666
- Ebook, Nook, Kindle, ISBN: 9781590955673
- Number of pages: 352
- Publication Date: 2013

Tidge Mackiewicz, new patriarch of his family, received several orders from his dying father, Kid Scream. One order stated that Tidge should quit believing in Santa Claus and stop acting like every day was Christmas. Tidge should also abandon his belief that the Luftwaffe shot down Santa Claus on Christmas Eve in 1944 and Santa survived.

Title: Heroes and Idles

- Author: Richard Baran
- Publisher: TotalRecall Publications, Inc.
- Paperback, ISBN:
- Ebook, Nook, Kindle, ISBN:
- Number of pages: 186
- Publication Date: 2016

A burlesque star, Indian Chief, two cantankerous grandfathers, an Italian grandmother who drinks whiskey from a Mason jar, a Prussian officer and a Chicago Cub baseball star impact four young lives.

Tess, Stan, Georgie and Gil had their idols. Tess worshipped her World War II era burlesque star, Aunt Rose and an Ojibwa Indian Chief, John Proud Bear in *Lunch with a Gypsy*. Georgie, a young father entangled in an affair, drew guidance from his immigrant Italian grandmother, Nana Beam's whiskey induced lessons about repentance in *I've Got a Secret*. Stan idolized his two cantankerous grandfathers and their lesson he learned about the real world. It was the death of his wife and then his mother that led him back to his high school sweetheart from four decades ago in *The One that Got Away*. Thirteen year old Gil had three heroes. His Poppy Paul taught him to respect his given name, Gilead. Gil's father formally introduced him to Wrigley Field the day after the Chicago Cubs traded Gil's third idol, Andy Pafko to the Brooklyn Dodgers. Tragically, death claimed Gil's father soon after and Gil later found a unique way to keep his dad's memory alive in *Trading Prushka*.

Title: Shutter Bug

- Author: Richard Baran
- Publisher: TotalRecall Publications, Inc.
- Paperback, ISBN: 9781590953167
- Ebook, Nook, Kindle, ISBN: 9781590953174
- Number of pages: 176
- Publication Date: 2016

Emma Grace Waveland, a self-proclaimed Shutter Bug at twelve, finds herself transported from a safari in Disney World to Africa's Serengeti where she joins a group of professional hunters who capture wild animals for zoos. Her new adventure brings her face-to-face with deadly crocodiles, a giant rhino, a python, a lady photographer who looks like a young version of her great grandmother, hunters who resemble old movie stars and a camp cook with mysterious powers. Her family doesn't believe her when she returns from her trip, but she has evidence on her cameras' memory cards and her iPhone.

**A Mouse Gate Adventure
Book What's your adventure?**

www.mousegate.com